I0670561

The *Bell* Ringer

A Collection Of Short Stories

The *Bell* Ringer

A Collection Of Short Stories

Collins Odhiambo

Copyright © 2013 Collins Odhiambo
ISBN: 978-9966-1693-3-4

All rights reserved

No part of this publication may be reproduced, distributed, or
transmitted in any form or by any means, or stored in any database
or retrieval system, without the prior written permission of the
author and Sahel Publishing Association.
The author assumes full responsibility for all content of this book

Published by Sahel Publishing Association,
a subsidiary of Sahel Books Inc.
P.O. Box 18007—00100
Nairobi, Kenya
Tel: +011-254-715-596-106
For questions and orders log on to:
www.sahelpublishing.net

A Sahel Book

Editor: Sam Okello

Interior designed by Hellen Wahonya Okello
Cover designed by Hellen Wahonya Okello
Printed in India, U.K., U.S.A.

I dedicate this book to my late grandfather Japheth Ogola Manyala, who predicted fame and greatness such as this and other created works of mine are bound to bring my way. He, surely, must share in what glory there is or will be for me.

Acknowledgement

My appreciations go to all who contributed directly or indirectly towards making this a tangible intellectual product now nourishing minds world-over. Among you may I just mention Dismas Ojow and Lilian Obunga, who separately read aloud my writings as soon as I had penned them, their voices bringing to life my fictional personalities as well as rendering lively the scenes and events thereof; all of you girls who eagerly read my stories in the manuscript form and enthusiastically narrated to me what you had read, hence motivating me to write even more; Elisha Otieno, whose energy and drive got a lot of things done expeditiously; and, perhaps above all, my publisher Sam Okello and his able team at Sahel Publishing Association, whose speed and efficiency in the publishing process truly amazed me.

TABLE OF CONTENTS

One

Three Little Friends

Once upon a time there occurred an acute famine in the wild world. The famine was occasioned by a prolonged draught which saw the earlier lush land change into a boring brownness that bespoke great distress to the inhabitants. Neither solution nor respite was in sight.

Now some small, clever and talented members of the wild world thought of a way to seek and bring help to their world. They were Mosquito, Bee and Spider. And where else could they go but to the palace of Omwami, the king of the human world?

On their way to the palace, the three little friends decided that they would present a sweet song to the king of the human world so as to please his heart and smooth the way for their pleas. Mosquito and Bee had very beautiful voices; Spider, at her very best, could sing off key. The gifted ones, however, encouraged the less gifted one, and when together they tried out a simple praise song, the harmony of their blended voices was great, except for certain points in the song that had particularly high notes which obviously troubled the less talented Spider. Mosquito suggested that at such points Spider should simply open her mouth in line with the syllables of the words concerned, without producing a sound. They tried out the song again. It pleased them even more. Excitedly, they ran about, round and round. Their song was sweet indeed. It would please the king of the human world.

Mosquito was still fat then, the size of her friend Bee. Spider still had wings. They had always liked each other very much. As a matter of fact, this was not the first thing the three of them were doing together. And in this time of dire need in their world, it could only be noble that they should use their skills in cooperation and teamwork to try and find a solution for the benefit of all. They were sure that this particular mission of theirs would bring salvation to their fellow inhabitants of the wild world, who actually were staring death in the face.

They flew on. Most of the time, Spider was in the middle, Bee to her right, and Mosquito to her left.

And when they felt tired, they flew low and finally landed on top of a tree in order to have a rest. Bee visited a few flowers and sucked their nectar while Mosquito and Spider descended to the ground to find some water, collected somewhere, which they could drink. After the deserved rest they got together and took to flight again. They journeyed on to the human world.

So there they were, before Omwami the king of the human world, who was taking a rest in the open, sipping away at his wine from a golden goblet, feet upon a footstool. The king welcomed them and showed them to a sofa near his own seat. They, however, did not sit. They told the king that they had a presentation for him first.

And just before they started the song, Spider left the line and stood in front of his friends so that he may conduct the singing. And Spider raised his limbs in the air and shaped his mouth in a manner ready to pronounce the first word of the first line of the song. Bee and Mosquito, being fast learners, understood what was happening, and so when Spider dropped his limbs in one motion, they attacked the song in wonderful harmony and with captivating power. Mosquito's great soprano and Bee's lovely alto were absolutely awesome in that presentation before Omwami the king of the human world. And the king was truly pleased.

And the king called them nearer to him, gave each a firm handshake and motioned them to the seat that he had shown them. The visitors sat, resting their backs on the velvety cushions of the sofa. And the king asked them their names, and each made a fitting introduction. Spider then moved on to explain to the king why exactly they had visited. He gave an account of the acute famine in the wild world. He observed that even though the human world too was experiencing the adverse effects of the prolonged lack of rain, humans at least had a number of advanced survival mechanisms unlike them of the wild world who were totally at the mercy of nature.

So the king said that he understood their situation and that he deeply sympathized with them and all their fellow inhabitants of the wild world. There and then, he undertook to send his men to take four big water tanks to the four corners of the wild world, fill each with water from the borehole in the palace compound, and ensure that those tanks always contained water. The three little friends felt happy about this. In their seated position, Mosquito and Bee each hit her three right limbs against the left ones in a manner of hearty clapping. Spider joined in the clapping, hitting her four right limbs against the left ones, but, apparently, he had thoughts in his mind which made his clapping to sound less hearty. But no – he was no less appreciative; Spider loved to express his feelings in words, and it was for the very best of these that his mind had begun searching, right from the moment the king had begun delivering the words of his generous promise to them and their needy world. And, indeed, Spider, in very colourful words, expressed his gratefulness to the king, on his own behalf, on behalf of his two compatriots in his company and on behalf of the entire wild world. And the king was greatly impressed, impressed by these visitors of his. They had, in fact, given him a different picture, a very different picture of the wild world as he had always known and viewed it. Now he knew for sure that something good could come out of the wild world, if what he had seen in these three little friends was anything to go by.

And the king asked the visitors to stay for lunch, after which they could start on their way back to their motherland. Meanwhile, he said to them, they would be shown around the palace, as lunch was getting ready.

And the visitors got to see many things. Spider kept right beside the king and watched the king's gestures and even movement of lips as he spoke explaining to them what was what there in the palace. They were shown framed pictures and wall clocks, cupboards and wall units, books and magazines, beds and bedding, cups and mugs, bowls and dishes and all. And the visitors even saw a television, and marvelled at the fact that small people, who looked like this king, were actually talking inside it. Having had lunch with the king, the visitors said bye to him and his people at the palace, expressing their gratefulness for everything, and especially the donations of water for their wild world. Then they set out on their way back to their motherland.

To Bee, that afternoon's heat was much less than the previous afternoon's and, indeed, all the others since the rains had disappeared. Excitedly she proposed that they sing, but her friends said that the journey was long and that singing was going to make them tired before they got home.

Spider now asked to be excused, for she was going for a long call. With a light touch he added that much was what they had eaten at the palace. Mosquito and Bee smiled and said that it was all right, and that they would wait for her at that spot. Spider, however, urged them just to go on at the normal pace; that she would catch up with them soon enough.

So Mosquito and Bee flew on slowly, smoothly and easily. A thought came to Bee's mind. If she got to their king in the wild world and said that it was she who had negotiated the bringing of water donations from the human world, their king would reward her handsomely. Brilliant! she thought to herself. She allowed the thought to ferment in her mind as she and Mosquito flew. Spider had not caught up with them as she had said she would, even though they had been flying so slowly all the way.

The two were now nearing the border of the human world and the wild world. Bee suggested to Mosquito that Mosquito should fly back, and where she would meet Spider, she should hold Spider's limb and help her fly faster in order that the three of them may enter their motherland together and together give their king the good news that they had successfully negotiated and got aid, in form of water, for their world.

So, Mosquito began flying back. She was tired all right, but Bee had persuasively urged her just to do it, that it was important and that Spider could not have been too far off anyway. But what Bee might not have known, even as she was putting forth such a calculated persuasion, was that Mosquito personally had been entertaining thoughts of going back and remaining in the human world. Mosquito had been so much fascinated by the human world. Indeed, Spider herself had this same desire, hers actually being completely overwhelming. And in telling her friends that she was going for a long call, Spider had just played a trick on them, so that she may get back to the palace in the human world, without his friends knowing exactly what was happening. And while her friends had been flying back home, thinking that she would be catching up with them soon enough, Spider had made her way back to the palace and charmed the king into granting her citizenship.

But before granting Spider human world citizenship, the king had required her to agree to losing her wings. That way, the king told her, she would not be flying easily to her native motherland and back to human world, as the human world did not allow dual citizenship. The king had, as well, told her that she would be using her natural silk thread to construct webs to trap small individuals who had no citizenship in the human world but would be entering it secretly and illegally. Spider had accepted that duty and undertaken to play it as a role – not just to do it as a duty.

And since Mosquito's heart had been won over by the experience of earlier that day, she had somehow mastered strength to fly all the way back to the human world. And here she now was, back to the human world. She was now very, very thin. Too much was the travelling that she had done on any given day. But it would not be a matter at all if she would get citizenship here in the human world.

Unfortunately for Mosquito, she could not persuade the king to grant her citizenship. The king saw no special useful role she could play in the human world, and he told her so. He told her this very politely but perfectly firmly too.

Mosquito's hunger and tiredness was now compounded by anger and disappointment. Fury raged inside her, inside that body of hers that had now become so thin. But even she knew that there was nothing she could do about the matter of citizenship if the king had rejected her request.

So Mosquito decided that she would not go back to the wild world. She would, instead, operate somewhere between these two worlds. That way, she would find opportune moments to enter the human world illegally and obtain a few benefits, chiefly the blood of the citizens of the human world.

That evening, Bee got a rousing welcome. The wild world honoured her. On behalf of all the citizens, their king awarded her the title 'Grand Hero of the Wild World'. She was allowed to establish a kingdom within the wild world, and to reign as its queen. Further, she was blessed, so that her sons should be the fiercest of soldiers in the whole wild world.

Spider, now a proud holder of human world citizenship, continued to live and move about freely wherever and whenever she pleased in that world. And because the king loved her, she continued to access even the king's wonderful bedroom. She would get beneath the bed, between the sheets, into the wardrobe – anywhere.

And Mosquito established the habit of illegal entry into the human world. While there, she unleashed her anger and disappointment at having been denied human world citizenship by not only sucking up the citizens' blood but also injecting into them things that made them ill. And to this day, Mosquito does this. Just before she takes human blood illegally, she always tries to sing the way she and her friends had once done to the king of the human world. She does not achieve the beauty of their then combined voices, but she sings well enough to soothe the citizens of human world, just before she pierces their skins and draws a little measure of blood – a little from one, a little from another, till she gets full for the night.

May I grow as tall as the tree at my uncle's home!

Two

The Bell Ringer

It was *chon gi lala*, long ago. There was a land far beyond the clouds. The land was called Polo. The rulers of Polo were twenty-four. No one had made these rulers; they had just come into existence, all at once, in the beginning of time. Thus they were equal. They were perfectly democratic. They did their things together, each ruler taking the task at which he was best. And they achieved great things this way. One such achievement, and of which they were particularly proud, was their bringing into being the land of Kakoth and all that was in it. The land of Kakoth was far below the clouds. They had made it, and they had made people and things and placed in it.

Chieng' had initially made a powerful torch which had lit Polo and enabled the rulers to see and to go about everything. He had made another big torch to light the land of Kakoth. Many other torches he had made, so that Kakoth may have light – even at night, to some degree. His fellow rulers regarded him as a genius, this ruler called Chieng'. How he made light they never could comprehend! Then there was Muya. He was an expert at gas-making. Muya was the Polo ruler who had come up with the chief gas that made life possible. Also, he had made a layer of gas just below Polo. This layer of gas, Muya had explained, would protect all things that had been made and placed in the land of Kakoth. All other gases were made by him. There was also a ruler called Koth. This Polo ruler had rainmaking talent. He had a profound understanding of the mechanism of rainmaking – this ruler called Koth! He often explained this mechanism to his fellow rulers but each time he had to end the explanation before he delivered even half of it, for the whole thing was incomprehensible to the other rulers. Anyway, rainmaking was his part; and he played this part excellently. He would go to Polo Hills and cause rain. The rest of the rulers always thought of him with kindness whenever they watched rain falling from Polo, showering the land of Kakoth far below the clouds. And Lowo, Le, Obok, and other rulers, also made things which each of them knew best.

Thus the rulers of Polo always were so proud of each other and each other's effort. And at their meeting place, an amphitheatre-like structure which they had named The Pantheon, good humour and wit prevailed. The Pantheon was the centre of creative thinking and serious planning. Just before the rulers left The Pantheon for their private abodes at the end of any given day, they would sing in sweet harmony. The words and sound of the song they sang would therefore linger in their thoughts, accompanying each to his private abode. One day, however, it happened that after a much productive session at The Pantheon, their sweet singing was not the last thing they heard. From without, there was a tintinnabulation, a powerful tintinnabulation. It reached all the four corners of Polo; so loud it was. Each ruler therefore went to his private abode wondering why a bell should ring and, most importantly, who the bell ringer might be. And about this, each of them kept thinking.

Morning came. The new day was spent. Another day began; and it, too, ended. Nothing out of the ordinary occurred. The rulers could not put the tintinnabulation out of their mind. Life continued though.

Now, Koth loved adventure. One day, he decided to descend to the land of Kakoth, the land far below the clouds. He wished to see for himself the practical benefits that his role was bringing to the inhabitants of the land below the clouds. So, Koth set out on that adventurous journey, the kind of which none of the other rulers had even thought of undertaking.

After a day and a half, he landed in the land of Kakoth, in the middle of a path that led to River Kakoth. He looked from side to side. The place looked strange. It was mostly green, unlike Polo, which was predominantly the colour cotton of wool.

Then Koth saw a being coming towards him from the direction of the river, the great River Kakoth, which was not very far off. The being had a barrel of water on the head, supported in place by the hands. Although this being was in every way like Woman, whom they had made in the beginning of time, she was more pleasant to look at, being so much younger.

She walked on. She got to where Koth was. Koth spread his arms so that she could not get past him.

So close and face to face with her now, his manhood began to rise, like the swelling of leavened bread. He liked her breasts, especially the way they now appeared, given that both of her arms were raised, holding in place the brim of the barrel that was on her head. Koth's eyes swept down her body, right to her legs, and then returned to her lips, which now twitched with tension resulting from being studied like that.

Koth spoke; and this relieved the tension.

"I am the maker of rain," he said.

"Where do you come from? I have never seen anyone like you here in Kakoth," said the young woman. Her voice pleased Koth.

"You are right," Koth said. "I have just landed right on this spot. I come from Polo, the land far beyond the clouds."

"Is that so? I mean – what are you doing here?"

"I decided to descend here to see for myself the beauty and fertility of this place."

"Ah, I see."

"And, having seen thee, I have seen all that is worth my coming here."

"Oh, come on. I – I do not know what you are talking about."

"Thy hair is fair, thy waist is supple. Thy breasts deserve a godly touch, thy tongue desires a game with mine."

"Oh, please. May I pass! My mum's waiting for this water."

"As I've just said, I am the maker of rain. I cause it to fall whenever and wherever I please."

And Koth took the barrel of water off the young woman's head. She had struggled with him a bit but had let him have his way. He poured it out on the ground beside them. The young woman stood akimbo, scowling.

"At the click of my fingers, rain shall fall so that everyone can fetch water conveniently," he said.

And Koth did the clicking of fingers. And rain began to fall. But it did not fall around where they stood. The young woman marvelled. Silence reigned between them.

"That's how we do it in Polo," said Koth, causing the young woman's attention to return to where they stood. She regarded Koth as though she was noticing him for the first time. He was very clean. He was handsome. His body was attractively built. His speech had such excellence as was beyond men.

He moved even closer to her. He took her hand. He then held her waist with both of his hands. She felt tickled by this touch. He now looked at her lips. More and more hungrily he looked at those ripe lips.

She parted her lips slowly. He saw this. He moved his mouth in the direction of hers and reached those ripe lips. He kissed them. Feelings stirred inside her. His tongue soon was touching hers pleasantly.

And Koth did with her the deed of pleasure upon that spot. They did this till the rain ceased.

Then they rose. A last hug he gave her.

Then Koth's feet left the ground. He was leaving the land of Kakoth. She watched him ascend. She wished that he had stayed longer in Kakoth.

Up and up he went. Smaller and smaller he got, till he disappeared in the clouds. And upon his disappearing, there was a tintinnabulation, the ringing of a bell. The sound seemed to her to be coming from the clouds where Koth had disappeared, and it reached her loudly and clearly. She stood still. The tintinnabulation ceased. All became calm. All became still. She started on her way home, with her empty water barrel.

And she told her family all that had happened. And it got to the neighbours. Like wild fire it spread and covered the whole of Kakoth, so that everyone knew of her encounter with a being from the land far beyond the clouds. She began being treated as a special one, for she had had contact with a ruler of Polo. And in her praise, the poet of Kakoth composed this:

> Brown one of our land
> In the low lying plains
> He who causes rains
> Came and sought your hand,
> Gave you godly seeds
> In you to sprout then grow to meet our needs.

And it was turned into song. And the people of Kakoth sang it every so often, in praise and honour of she who had charmed a ruler of the land far beyond the clouds.

In the land far beyond the clouds, Koth found out that quite a few things had changed. His travel to and from the land below the clouds had taken just three days yet so much had changed back home.

It was that Chieng' had proposed in The Pantheon that Polo needed one of its twenty-four rulers to be the supreme leader, adding that he would humbly accept to be such a leader if he received the endorsement of the majority.

The proposition indeed was cracking the brains of the rulers of Polo. Koth had found Muya and Lowo in particularly deep thought. They were carefully considering the validity of the idea of one supreme leader. They would then go into the question of who among them would be best suited for the position of Supreme Ruler, should it be created.

Well, the idea looked attractive, especially if one imagined oneself in the proposed position.

So it was decided in The Pantheon that the position of Supreme Ruler was thereby created.

Muya offered himself for the created position of Supreme Ruler. He argued that being the owner of breath, which sat at the very core of the principle of life itself, he was best suited for the supreme position. Muya received a sizable following upon that declaration.

So in The Pantheon, one afternoon, it was that Koth had also thrown his hat in the ring. In offering himself as a candidate, he said that his rainmaking ability was supremely important since it was what sustained all created life. And as a well-travelled person, who enjoyed great good will even among the people of the land below the clouds, he, more than anyone else, deserved the position of Supreme Ruler, he said. He too got a good following.

And when that day the rulers had finished their business in The Pantheon, they sang in harmony. Immediately the song ended, there was tintinnabulation, a ringing of the bell. For a whole minute the bell rang. When it ceased, the rulers left for their private abodes. Each thought of why a bell should be ringing and who the bell ringer was, and where the bell ringer was, and what the bell ringer was up to!

Well, in a matter of weeks it became clear that Chieng', Muya and Koth were the serious contenders for the position of Supreme Ruler. Lowo had fronted himself, but he had shelved his ambitions, choosing to throw his weight behind Koth. While bowing out, he had said that even though his role was vital, just as that of any of his fellow rulers, he was convinced that Koth was first among equals.

And there were divided loyalties in The Pantheon. Rulers sat by the side of the one whom they supported. Supporters would walk their preferred candidate to his private abode, in the course of which they discussed strategies for winning the Supreme Ruler post.

In the land far below the clouds, the young woman whom Koth had known had since given birth to twin boys. Although human, they had their father's godly abilities. They were interesting. They were just little fat children but they understood what adults said to them and they already influenced life. They were already making rain.

So the twin rainmakers were consulted widely. From all over the land of Kakoth, people came to the home of 'Mother of Rain' so that her boys could help them. With different problems they came to the home of 'Mother of Rain'. Some who had delayed in beginning to plough, and could not plant when the big rains fell, now asked the boys to let rain fall only upon the parts of the farms that they had cultivated. This way, they said, they could plant as they continued to plough.

The twin rainmakers of Kakoth did quite well, though they often used their powers corruptly. They would seek and accept bribes so as to influence rains. As a matter of fact, they influenced rains in such a way that even the established rainfall patterns were disrupted. Jealous individuals would ask them to keep rain from falling on certain farms. Accompanying such a request would be offers that were too attractive for the rainmakers to resist. And from Polo, Koth came to notice that there would be rain in the land below the clouds even without him causing it, and that equally often there would be no rain in spite of his going to Polo Hills and actually applying his rainmaking procedure. He wondered why this was so.

The rulers of Polo were about to hold elections to the office of Supreme Ruler. Muya had since quit the race. He had told The Pantheon that after careful reflection and deep thought, he had arrived at the conclusion that Chieng' was best placed to serve in the office of Supreme Ruler. Chieng', he said, had a 'supreme enabling power' which when he released, all things became possible. He added that if anything, were it not for Chieng', Polo rulers could not have even started any of the projects, the projects in whose successful completion they all took singular pride.

By that evening, opinion leaders said, the race was tight. Koth was leading by a very narrow margin, a lead attributed to Koth's jovial personality.

And when all was said and done that day, the rulers sang in harmony in readiness to leave The Pantheon. Immediately the song was over, there was a tintinnabulation. For a whole minute the bell rang. The rulers then went their separate ways, disturbed, of course.

The following day, it was said that Chieng' had edged out Koth in popular opinion, taking a slim lead. It emerged that there was a scandal to which this turn of events could be attributed. It is this scandal that came to be known as 'Mother of Rain Scandal'.

The land beyond the clouds was shocked to learn that Koth had descended to the land of Kakoth and known a young woman carnally, and that he had kept it all secret all that while.

It was Muya who had unearthed this scandal. Muya explained that he had travelled down towards the clouds for a breath of fresh air just after bowing out of the rather grueling race for the office of Supreme Ruler. From that position, he reported, he had observed much jubilation in the land below the clouds, the cause of which he sought to find out. For this reason he had descended there. And there he learnt of the deeds of Koth, every detail of what Koth did there. A massive statue had even been erected at the home of the woman whom Koth had known carnally. She had died some months after delivering twins. The people of a Kakoth had erected a statue in her honour, a statue they had named 'Mother of Rain'. To that site the people went once every month to pay homage. At the foot of the massive statue they sang 'Brown One of the Land' and said passionate prayers.

Koth had responded to his opponents. An astute politician, he sought to turn the so called Mother of Rain Scandal to his advantage. He said that the people of the land below the clouds were free to show love, honour and appreciation to anyone, especially one of their own; that only a dictator could see such expression of freedom as a bad thing. In this regard, he undertook to defend and protect fundamental freedoms in Polo if he got elected the Supreme Leader. As to his having descended to the land below the clouds, Koth had said that unlike his main challenger, Chieng', who was aloof, he was a leader who had a great sense of common touch. He said he was well known as someone who maintained close contact with everyone, hence his popularity everywhere. The candidate emphasized that Polo could not be well if the land of Kakoth was not well, and that it was in this spirit that he had decided to make a visit there, something that his opponents had turned into political mud to sling at him. He laughed at his opponents' level of appreciation of foreign affairs, given that they found visits outside Polo so objectionable. And addressing the matter of intercourse with a young woman in the land far below the clouds, Koth said that such an allegation was a clear demonstration of the desperation of his opponents; that the alleged intercourse was nothing but the figment of imagination of some pretentious Polo ruler who harboured lustful desires. On this note he openly challenged Muya to give the inhabitants of Polo an honest account as to his recent travel to the land of Kakoth. He challenged him to talk of his encounter with the daughters of Kakoth when he descended there ostensibly to breathe fresh air. Koth asserted that he was a clean ruler, literally and in personal conduct.

And that vigorous defence of himself gave him back the lead. Quite a few in The Pantheon decamped to his side as the appointed hour of election approached.

Then when The Pantheon convened the following day to have the election to the office of Supreme Ruler, when all twenty-four Polo rulers had got everything ready and were ready to begin the casting of votes, the bell rang. It was not the rather distant tintinnabulation they had from time to time heard. The bell rang with deafening intensity. And it rang nonstop. And the more they waited for the ringing to cease, the more intense it got, so that none could stay in The Pantheon.

So they all got out, and the ringing was getting stronger, as if it was following them. And their eardrums could not take any more of the ringing. And they ran off. In different directions the rulers ran, the ringing bell driving them away. They stumbled and fell, but got up and picked up speed. And far away from the ringing bell they ran, leaving The Pantheon kilometers behind them. And still they ran, each in his own direction.

And as they ran to comfort, the bell ringer now spoke above the weakening tintinnabulation. The bell ringer said that everything was already fixed and needed neither intervention nor interference from supreme self-seekers. Said the bell ringer: "The torches that light the land below the clouds will continue to shine, and regularly. The rain shall fall when it has formed, and this will happen in regular patterns as long as no man interferes with its formation. Air will remain abundant; it is upon those who breathe it to keep it clean…"

And the sound of the bell grew weaker and weaker, and what the bell ringer said had now become hard for the ear to perceive and discriminate distinctively.

A few days after, the rulers went back to The Pantheon. They did not revive the matter of election nor entertain the idea of Supreme Ruler itself. They discussed other matters of their land, land beyond the clouds. Then they sang in harmony and left The Pantheon. The bell did not ring. The words of the song they had sung lingered in their minds, accompanying them to their private abodes.

And life went on. And the bell ringer ensured that nothing was again left to chance. And the bell now mostly tolled, as opposed to the earlier furious tintinnabulation which, on occasion, would threaten to send the Polo rulers deaf. And the tolling of the bell would be perceived only by those for whom the bell ringer had a piece of communication. And in the very early hours of each new day, the bell ringer's bell tolled to remind cocks in the land far below the clouds to crow so as to herald the dawn. And it tolled to the donkey too, reminding it to let out a bray in those wee hours of the morning. And when the big torch that lit the day was ready to cast a yellow-orange suffusion of light into the eastern horizon, while it was yet low and behind the far eastern hills of Kakoth, the bell ringer's bell tolled to the birds of the air, and the birds sounded the dawn chorus. And at intervals in the course of the shining of the big torch that lit the day, the bell ringer's bell would toll to remind the cocks to crow; and the people of the land of Kakoth could tell the time from the cocks' crowing. When the rainy season approached, the bell ringer's bell would toll to remind certain birds that flew in a large group to fly above the land of Kakoth; and when the people of Kakoth beheld the gray-breasted birds fly over them in that spectacular fashion, they would know that the rainy season had come.

Once in a while, rulers of the land beyond the clouds felt an urge to assert their personal power in a more prominent fashion. Chieng', for example, would cause the big torch which he had made for the night, to block the light of the big torch of the day. And sometimes he would cause the big torch of the day to block the light of the big torch of the night. And when the inhabitants of the land far below the clouds saw the lights so blocked, they looked at the big torches above them and marveled and feared. The bell ringer would get concerned, and soon ring his bell and rebuke Chieng'. Chieng' would stop the act of mischief and the big torches would send down their lights as usual.

Koth too would seek to assert his power and influence. And when the land far below the clouds would be receiving rain, Koth would do a few tricks and turn the whole thing into a deluge, massive floods which hurt the people of the land below the clouds. Sometimes he did these little tricks of his and held back the rain when its time or season had come. The bell ringer, however, would ring the bell angrily, and Koth would just have to stop all that.

Lowo would cause the land of Kakoth to shake; and the people of Kakoth would wonder why the tables in their living rooms were shaking, beds squeaking, rocks rolling down from raised grounds, walls developing cracks, buildings crumbling to the ground or the waters of the Sea of Kakoth suddenly and forcefully sweeping through the coast, destroying whatever was there, killing the dwellers there. Lowo's shaking the land of Kakoth was the single most irksome act that the bell ringer had to deal with; for, Lowo did this very frequently. The bell ringer was always on the alert, and so, mostly, Lowo's shaking the land of Kakoth resulted but in a tremor or something completely imperceptible.

And even in the land far below the clouds, there were those who sought to exercise their personal power. The twin rainmakers in the land of Kakoth had since sired sons, and these sons could influence rains, and they could influence rains even to the detriment of the land. The bell ringer kept watch and acted to protect the people, the people of the land below the clouds.

There, as well, were very clever young men in the land of Kakoth. And they had extraordinary understanding of gases, just like the Polo ruler called Muya. And these clever ones made a certain gas that could kill all the dwellers of the land below the clouds within no time at all. And the bell ringer was alarmed, and there was a tintinnabulation, and these clever ones could not use this lethal gas which they had made. The bell would ring with deafening intensity when they so much as thought of using that lethal gas.

Ordinary individuals in the land of Kakoth themselves would catch created things in the Sea of Kakoth, catch these in order to sell them. Many of these sea creatures would be threatened with extinction. The bell ringer would ring the bell and the people who caught the creatures would leave them alone. The people of Kakoth would also cut down trees for many and various purposes, almost leaving the land of Kakoth deficient of these, almost bare. The bell ringer would ring the bell, cautioning that they should stop it. An individual would be doing something really worthwhile but then the individual would spend extra time on such a thing. And when the bell ringer judged that enough time had been spent on something, the bell ringer rang the bell.

And that is how it was, so long ago in the land far beyond the clouds and in the created land far below the clouds!

May I grow as tall as the tree at my uncle's home.

Three

Sun and Wind

Once upon a time Sun and Wind were great rivals. The two hardly ever missed an opportunity to quarrel or brag about what one of them could do but which the other could not. Many were the times they actually abandoned their assigned duties just to engage in personal taunting. On one occasion, for instance, Sun bragged to Wind that he was capable of giving orders from his seat, and, just like that, what he wished should happen, would happen exactly. Wind on the other hand, he said, had to move about personally and use unnecessary force if anything he wished done was to take place at all. And in response, Wind said that he could operate both at night and during the day. He told Sun that Sun was unadventurous, dull and boring; that he just sat at the same place as if he were a slave or something. And just to prove this, Wind had come out at night, blown about harshly, thereby uprooting a number of big trees in Kakoth, which he caused to lie down, their roots bearing soil, facing east from where Sun would emerge in the morning to behold the chaotic sight. And when Sun came out, as was routine, he indeed beheld the huge trees, including a *siala* tree that had attained admirably great heights, lying miserably where they had once stood proudly. Of course, Wind was right there to confirm that it was he who had done that. So Sun was very moody that particular morning. And Wind noticed his rival's low spirits and started blowing about over the land of Kakoth, as a victorious braggart would do. Wind went wild with excitement. He lifted women's dresses all of a sudden, exposing them so embarrassingly. He carried off clothes that had been aired without pegs, whirled them about in the space and then hurled them to the ground. Women cursed him aloud: "Lucifer! Satan! What brings you here? They shouted themselves hoarse, cursing him some more: "Your mother's buttocks!" They complained to each other in great annoyance at being exposed and at having to rinse clothes afresh. As all this went on, Sun now hid his face behind the clouds, almost completely. And there he admitted to himself that unlike Wind he could only stamp his authority during the day. He further noted to himself that even though he was very powerful, actually more powerful than Wind, his weight never could be felt as instantaneously as that of Wind. And so long as this was the case, Wind would always be deemed more powerful than he. He continued hiding behind the clouds, his ego terribly bruised by Wind's open challenge to him.

Then Sun hatched a thought. His face brightened up there behind the clouds, for he felt nice about the new idea. And thus he allowed the land of Kakoth to see his face again. And here is the idea that hatched in the mind of Sun. He had seen two brothers down in the land of Kakoth. They were dressed in exactly the same way – a black suit and white shirt and a black wide-brimmed hat. One was accompanying the other to his in-laws' place on the other side of the great hill of Kakoth, known locally as Got Kakoth. Two other young men had actually gone before them, leading cattle to the same place, cattle meant for bride price. Now, among the people of Kakoth sons-in-law were dignified individuals, and no less than perfect decorum was expected of them. Remaining neat in one's dressing was part of this dignity. So Sun challenged wind to a contest in which the winner would be hailed as 'The One-Who-Caused-a-son-in-law-to-Change-His-Dressing'.

Wind welcomed the challenge. As a matter of fact, he laughed at Sun, wondering why Sun was proposing a contest that he knew very well he could not win.

So now the brothers were on their way to their in-laws' place. It was approaching midday. Got Kakoth lay quite some distance ahead of these two young men. They would do their trekking till they got to the hill and show it their backs, literally. They would do a few more miles and then reach their destination.

All of a sudden, Wind blew very powerfully, causing the brothers' coats to flap wildly like flags in a strong wind. Actually the coat of the main man, the son-in-law himself, got torn along a stitch that held the three-piece material in place. This, however, did not have him alter his attire. They walked on, now clutching on to their coats, lest they should be caught unawares again.

Sun seemed not to be trying out anything. And this gave Wind reason to try out more tricks. His rival clearly was deficient of ideas, he thought to himself.

And Wind now decided that he should steal the wide-brimmed hats of the brothers, in one quick and fierce sweep, and fly them far off. That way, the brothers would get to their destination differently dressed from the way they had been upon leaving home.

Wind blew abruptly and forcefully so as to snatch the brother's hats. Unfortunately for him, the hats were held in place with strings that looped across the wearer's throat to the other side.

So Wind surrendered. He ran out of ideas, as it were.

And Sun spoke to Wind. "No more ideas?" he said, gently touching his forefinger on his head. Wind looked at him in annoyance, saying no word in reply.

"In ten minutes' time I'm causing the men to alter their dressing. You just watch this space," Sun added.

And the heat of the day became unbearable to the neatly dressed brothers. And the brothers took off their hats. Sun duly claimed victory; and Wind had nothing to say about it.

But this was the last time that Sun and Wind engaged in such battles of superiority. The rulers of Polo did not like the fact that as a result of the rivalry between these two, they often neglected their assigned roles and, worst of all, caused destruction, embarrassment and great inconvenience to the inhabitants of Kakoth. Just because of their egos! Therefore, the rulers of Polo summoned the two and talked to them. They urged them to do everything in their power to stop the unhealthy rivalry. And the two promised the rulers of Polo that they would stop their unhealthy rivalry. And from that day, whenever Sun is sending its rays down to the land of Kakoth, Wind gives him time to do so, and may only blow softly and smoothly once after quite some while in the process. And when Wind is on a serious mission, such as to carry rain to or away from the land of Kakoth, Sun must disappear to give Wind time to play its role.

May I grow as tall as the tree at my uncle's home!

Four

Mang'ong'o

River Kakoth never ever went dry. Even in this fierce draught, the harshest in the history of the land of Kakoth, it still flowed on, albeit only quietly and smoothly now. Its usual uproarious bubble, which would force those conversing in its vicinity to raise their voices to levels of shouts, was now not there. Its crystal clear waters, now of much reduced volume, allowed the river bed to be seen. It was smooth and lovely there, underneath the water. Nyaraka admired it all. She had just fetched this river's water into her green pail, placed the pail upon the bank and then returned to behold the lovely river bed. The patterns upon the river bed reminded her of her mother's earthen floor, recently mudded and beautifully decorated by skillful etching of patterns thereon with spiny succulent cactus leaves. Nyaraka envied the river bed. She wished that her body should receive a smooth touch, such as what the river bed was receiving from the smoothly flowing crystal clear water.

Upon turning so as to go and load her green pail of water onto her head, Nyaraka was shocked to realise that the pail was nowhere to be seen. She looked around in perplexity. The quiet of the early morning changed from serene to eerie. She felt as if every strand of her hair stood erect upon her head. What exactly had just happened?

Just then she heard female voices in conversation coming to the river. The tension in her eased but only somewhat. She already felt the awkwardness of having to

40

explain to people that her pail of water had disappeared mysteriously. How could a pail of water just disappear, Nyaraka already could figure the women questioning her upon her giving them such an illogical account.

The conversing women drew nearer. One of them let off a whoop of laughter; no doubt she had found truly amusing whatever it was that had just been said. Their morning merry sharply contrasted Nyaraka's present worry.

And when the women now caught sight of Nyaraka, they all adopted looks of familiar surprise. "Someone had already reached the river!" each seemed to be saying inwardly.

"Doesn't this daughter of Magwar sleep?" one of the women posed rhetorically, giving voice to their silent questions. The others just sighed. It was well known to them that Nyaraka, daughter of Magwar, was an early riser, a quality much prized in a daughter of Kakoth. Such, it was held, would make an excellent wife and mother, who would be getting things done in good time, as opposed to the kind who clang to the warm hug of the blanket till the sun's rays were strong enough to provide alternative warmth.

Before word could be exchanged between Nyaraka and the women, a melodious male voice began to sing on the other bank of the river:

> Nya nya nya Nyaraka Nyaraka nya nya nya
> Nyaraka Nyaraka nya nya nya
> I love you Nyaraka I love you nya nya nya
> I want you, to kiss you, to warm you nya nya nya
> To keep you to feed you Nyaraka nya nya nya

And the singing voice pleased not only Nyaraka, but also the other women. The singing voice, emanating from the bush on the other bank, became more and more pleasant by the seconds.

Nyaraka started crossing the river towards the singing voice, a voice she found absolutely irresistible. The other women watched her from a distance. The singing took away their breath, and held them in thrall. Never before had they listened to such.

And when Nyaraka reached the middle of the river, the vastness of the river filled her with fear. She looked back and beckoned the women, who were watching her from the bank. The women responded as Nyaraka desired. They stepped into the water in response to Nyaraka's unspoken plea for support. The river volume was low; they merely needed to draw their dresses to the middle of their thighs. And they waded to where Nyaraka was. And their coming along now gave Nyaraka courage, much courage.

The singing got even more pleasant. Oh, that voice! It was better than the voice of the best singer in the whole of Kakoth. Nyaraka and the women now could hear the singer's passionate breathing as he called the name 'Nyaraka' in the song. Nyaraka's heart melted. She placed her open palm upon her breast and looked at the women in her company. The women marvelled. All of them wondered who the extraordinary singer might be.

On they waded, across the wide River Kakoth. They eventually got to the other side of the river. They released their dresses, which fell to their feet.

Oh, the women were not going to cross back to the other bank without laying eyes on the marvellous singer. And so they followed Nyaraka closely behind as Nyaraka moved into the bush where the singing voice emanated. Trees were of great height and together they formed multiple canopies. Climbing plants hugged stems and their tendrils entwined twigs just to make sure the support they had been granted was with them for life. Bush rope stood out in this. Rising but a few feet from the ground, and equally determined to be at their best, were the primroses, rhododendrons and *Dombea*. Nyaraka and the women made one step at a time through the vegetation. Of course, their eyes did the bulk of the work in this endeavour to find and behold the charming singer.

And they now caught sight of him! He was good-looking. Nyaraka's green pail was placed upon his laps nicely, like a baby upon its mother's laps. It was full of water, and a calabash floated in an inverted position on the surface of the water in the pail. And he sang on, beckoning them closer. And closer to Mang'ong'o Nyaraka and the women came.

And Mang'ong'o took the pail off his laps and placed it aside, on the ground. His singing got smoother and smoother as he now rose to meet Nyaraka and the women. And Nyaraka and the women felt no fear, for Mang'ong'o's voice bore only goodness and love, never a trace of harm.

But when Mang'ong'o had so enticed Nyaraka and the women to his vicinity, he transformed all of a sudden. He gained in girth and stature. His face developed an extra pair of eyes, and three horns sprouted on his head, two facing in front and the other backwards. A very long tail grew very fast from his hind quarters!

Mang'ong'o opened his mouth. There were no teeth. Only a wide red tongue, wet with saliva, dangled about therein. The sight of this paralised the women with trepidation. They fell to the ground in such great fear; but Nyaraka remained standing.

Mang'ong'o stretched his neck, and with his tongue he rolled the fallen women into his mouth, and swallowed the three of them greedily. Nyaraka observed the swallowed women rolling down Mang'ong'o's throat, and down towards his stomach.

An extraordinary sense of courage came to Nyaraka. "You will not swallow me," she said looking straight into Mang'ongo's eyes.

"Ha ha haaa!"Mang'ong'o laughed derisively. "I love brave women," he said in a raspy voice that was totally different from the one that had sang so sweetly up to just a while before.

"I know you love me, and that is why you will not swallow me," Nyaraka said, wearing upon her face something of a seductive expression.

But not even this piece of feminine skill in persuasion was going to stop Mang'ong'o. He looked at Nyaraka in silence. Nyaraka could see the swallowed women already settled in Mang'ong'o's stomach. Her courage ebbed. She felt like screaming, but she just could not bring herself to doing so.

Mang'ong'o opened his mouth. He wagged his wide tongue about. He stretched his neck towards Nyaraka. He licked Nyaraka's right cheek, and then her chin and forehead. This disgusted Nyaraka! She felt like slapping him but restrained herself. She stood there as helpless as any person could be.

Mang'ong'o faced away from Nyaraka and licked his lips gleefully. Then he raised his front legs in the air, opened his mouth, took in Nyaraka by the head and swallowed her.

And Nyaraka rolled down Mang'ong'o's throat, and down towards his stomach. Mang'ong'o yawned with satisfaction once Nyaraka had settled inside him. Then he lay there in the bush, well satisfied for the day. Hours passed. He continued lying there.

Meanwhile, Mrs Magwar had since become worked up owing to much worry over her daughter's whereabouts. With a mother's unerring instincts, she had long sensed that something was amiss. She had sensed this just minutes after the time she had expected to see Nyaraka getting through the gate, the green pail balanced beautifully upon her head as usual. And when Magwar had got back home from their maize and sorghum farm up the hill where he had been mending the fence, his wife had expressed her worry about Nyaraka but he had responded that his wife needed not worry unduly about a girl of Nyaraka's age, as it was never strange for even the most dutiful of girls to take time once in a while on things other than routine errands and chores. His wife had cursed him silently for displaying such a casual attitude towards the safety of a child.

Now when three men arrived in Magwar's compound to share their worry concerning the whereabouts of their wives, who had left home in the morning to go and fetch water in the river, Magwar took the matter more seriously, as his daughter too was nowhere to be seen or heard of.

The four men therefore turned themselves into a search party. They were determined to find their wives and the young Nyaraka. It was approaching the twelfth hour since the dawn of that day. Shadows were now very long. The sun, indeed, had done its diurnal journey above the land of Kakoth and was now about to go to rest in the west.

The four men got to the site of the river where women fetched water. The waters of River Kakoth flowed quietly downstream. Only some little bird could be heard letting off some sharp squeaky chirp at regular intervals, calling the attention of a mate or some close kin of its. No one was at the river apart from the four men. They walked along the bank of the river, both upstream and downstream. They got back to the point where they had begun.

Now one of them suggested that they cross to the other side. Everyone understood that there was no way they could return without their wives and daughter. So, quickly they bent and folded up their trousers to just above their knees. Their legs were truly the legs of the men of Kakoth – thin and quite hairy. Anyway, they started for the other bank of the wide river, Magwar taking the lead.

No sooner had they crossed over to the other bank than they heard a boy calling out: "Uncle Eli, come and see!"

Magwar caught sight of the boy. He had a pale skin. His lips were thin and pink. His hair was long and blond and tied in pony tail. He looked like no other boy he had seen in the entire land of Kakoth. Wonders of life!

And the one who was being called appeared, a young man who had the very features of the strange boy. "Andy, we've got to get back," the young man said to the boy.

Magwar turned and looked at his companions in near bewilderment. It was not enough that the strangers looked utterly different from the people of Kakoth; they as well spoke a language different from the language of Kakoth!

Magwar ventured to wave his hand to the strangers. The strangers responded through a similar gesture, much to Magwar's relief. The boy had a rifle slung over his left shoulder.

The boy pointed to his companion something that apparently was just beyond where they stood. Amazement was obvious in the way they stood looking at whatever it was.

Magwar too got sight of it. It was a massive creature! It was lying with its head rested on the trunk of a big fallen tree, its four big eyes closed. Magwar motioned his companions to move closer and see it too. The creature lazily opened one of its four big eyes. Its white eyeball rolled as it took a look at the human beings who were moving close to it. The men with Magwar turned and made to run away; but they fell down after hardly a step. Magwar was afraid but the courage of the two strangers drove away most of his fear, so he kept his eyes on the monstrous creature.

Magwar beheld with wonder as the boy held his riffle, aiming it at the creature that had scared the hell out of them, these men of Kakoth. And the boy's riffle released three bullets in quick succession. The bullets got right to their target: the head of the massive creature. And the massive creature threw itself in the air, and then fell to the ground with a thud. In no time at all it lay dead. And the young man who was with the boy unsheathed a sword that he took from where it was held round its waist. And with the sword the young man sliced open the belly of the massive creature. Nyaraka and the three women of Kakoth came out of the belly of the massive creature! They were tired, hungry and dirty. Nyaraka was the first to come out. In great disgust she clicked her tongue at the massive creature. She spat on the ground. She spat again.

So the four men of Kakoth took their women and daughter home. And they told the people of Kakoth all that they had witnessed and experienced during that search, combining it with the account of the earlier part of the day as narrated by Nyaraka and the three women on their way home that evening.

And this story became an unwritten law in the land of Kakoth: that never should one go to the river too early or too late, especially alone. The story came to be known as Mang'ong'o; and it spread throughout the land of Kakoth. Everyone who heard it for the first time rushed to Magwar's place to hear it first-hand. The other three men's homesteads also saw people coming in to hear the story, but it was Magwar's homestead that everyone naturally felt had the very core of the story, one of the strangest stories ever heard in the land of Kakoth.

And as it had been, the young man who had slit open Mang'ong'o's belly had handed his sword to Magwar as a gift, just after Magwar had given a word of thanks before crossing back to the other bank with dear ones who had been rescued from Mang'ong'o. And when he had given Magwar the sword that had recovered his daughter for him, Magwar had felt very strongly that he should promise the stranger the hand of Nyaraka in marriage, but his instincts had warned him against this, for he knew nothing about the young man beyond his having got him back his Nyaraka. He would, however, cherish and revere the sword.

And it was right under Magwar's bedding that he kept the sword that had been given to him by the strange young man that evening. The sword was to be passed from one generation to the next.

But as fate would have it, Nyaraka felt indescribable love for the stranger who had got her out of the belly of Mang'ong'o the massive creature. Every dawning day Nyaraka daughter of Magwar craved the young man who had got her out of the massive Mang'ong'o's belly. The more the story of Mang'ong'o got told in the land of Kakoth the more Nyaraka became oppressed with unexpressed love for this young man who had saved her. So one day, weeks after the unfortunate day, Nyaraka saw the young man who had saved her. It was about midday. He had brought his cows to drink at the water-drawing spot on River Kakoth. And Nyaraka knelt and thanked the rulers of Polo for bringing her saviour to her again. From the other bank of River Kakoth the young man watched her actions and understood her deep love for him. He crossed over to where Nyaraka was. Nyaraka led him home, where she declared to her parents that she had decided to take the young man to be her husband. She eagerly told her parents, who, of course, were yet uneasy about the whole thing, that she had even learnt how to say a few things in the young man's language, that the young man and his people were just as human as the people of Kakoth after all.

And Nyaraka's parents gave in to this overwhelming power of love, love that was evident in Nyaraka's movement, manner of speech, facial expression, dreams and everything else about her.

So Nyaraka became the very first daughter of Kakoth to marry outside the land of Kakoth. The people of Kakoth found this truly strange, but deep down they knew that the happenings surrounding Nyaraka's life were no ordinary ones. Hers was a life under the control of the rulers of Polo, they concluded.

And from then on, a house or any house-like structure constructed anywhere in the land of Kakoth would have a stick curved into the shape of a sword sticking sharply from the top of the roof, in symbolic memory of the salvation which the strange young man had brought a daughter of the land of Kakoth. The stick pointing sharply in the direction of Polo was, as well, to keep the memory of Nyaraka in every Kakoth home, Nyaraka the fair maiden whom Polo rulers had chosen from among the people of Kakoth to go and live in a world virtually unknown to the people of Kakoth.

And that was how it was – so long ago in the land of Kakoth.

May I grow as tall as the tree at my uncle's home.

Five

At the Well

It was quiet and calm, the midday sun openly cruel. Jopus, nearly frazzled after miles of trekking, trudged towards the well at Kakoth. Whereas his friends had branched to the local shopping centre in order to get themselves some snacks, Jopus himself had walked straight ahead and then branched to the well, the well at Kakoth.

Now, it was not for nothing that that Jopus had come to this well. He had done his homework well; hence he was sure that Pam would be here at this hour. He stood by, waiting, a blade of grass held across his mouth between his incisors.

Pam appeared. She seemed to be in foul mood, actually going past Jopus without so much as a 'hi'. She descended the gentle gradient into the well. She placed her pail near the water. She drew her skirt up her thighs, holding it in place with her left hand lest it should touch and absorb water. The other hand held a calabash. With this she fetched water, transferring the same into the yellow pail. She bent, fetched and transferred; bent, fetched and transferred. Jopus watched her. He liked what he was beholding. Those legs! They were already great below the knees – being so smooth, so brown, so shapely. The exposed part above the knees therefore now excited Jopus very much. It seemed to him as if he was looking at a ripe mango flesh sliced with a knife. His tongue licked his lower lip with desire. All the while Pam bent, fetched and transferred water into her pail.

Jopus cleared his throat so as to be granted attention. Pam turned her head in his direction, her left hand yet holding onto her drawn-up skirt.

"Woman," he said, "give me some water to drink. I feel thirsty and hot."

"Since when did my tribe share water with yours?" she said, her eyes fixed to the water of the well, an air of insouciance obvious in her manner.

"If you knew who asks you for water, such would not be the question you ask," he said.

"Your accent and strong physique are characteristic of our enemy tribe."

"You certainly are a keen woman; keen and conscious of things. Yet all I want is your water – not your tribe's."

"My water?"

"Yes, woman. I'm hot and thirsty; very thirsty for your water."

"Ha! You are just as all the men I've known. I know what you want."

"Many are the men you've known – this I know."

"What are you talking about?"

"Yes, you think that I am about to be your seventh man."

"How did you know such a thing about me?"

"Oh, it matters much to you."

"How…"

"If you will but give me your water under the shade yonder, I shall tell you every detail about yourself."

"Are you serious, sir?"

"I do not look otherwise, do I?"

And so Pam placed her calabash inside the pail that was now half-full of water. She stepped from the stone upon which she had stood fetching water. She ascended out of the well. Jopus took her hand as he pointed out to her where they were to go. He bid her walk in front. She did so. He followed closely behind, of course, studying her body. Their conversation was only light, obviously meant only to keep away any awkward tension while they moved to the shade of the giant fig tree.

They got there. Green grass carpeted the ground around the giant tree – just as if it were some great soccer pitch, say in England (the shade perhaps making this place superior). There sat Jopus and Pam, side by side, the way lovers do in city parks.

This was the day. Jopus had always longed for such a situation since this woman once caught his attention during one of his missionary tours here in Kakoth. He had back then spotted her with a man he had then counted truly lucky to have such a woman for a life companion. That man had since died. Pam was still on the rebound – well a tragic sort of rebound but rebound all the same. He, Jopus, needed to be there for her at her point of great need, when the misery of being alone and lonely could very well cause further tragedy. This was the day and the hour. Emotion ran through Jopus. It was the nervousness just before a major move.

"As you give me your water, woman, I'll give you mine," began Jopus. "And, in drinking my water, you never will thirst again," he added with passion, moving Pam's emotions, so that she made up her mind to give him her water, withholding none of it from him. She gave him. Nestlings atop the giant tree witnessed it all. Falling fig leaves too witnessed it.

When he had drunk – and she, too, had drunk – they rose and went and sat at the edge of the shade. They held out to each other's nose the flowers they had plucked and given to each other while they were moving here at the edge of the shade. The scent pleased them. From this position they could see the well. It was as they had left it.

They looked into each other's face and giggled. Pam adopted a seriousness of face. Jopus looked harder at her. Her face relaxed into a smile, a very bright smile. Jopus' further staring made her lips twitch with shyness. No man had looked at her so deeply before, so penetratingly that she could feel the contents of her heart and mind invaded and laid bare.

"What?" said Pam concerning how she was being looked at.

"Come here," said Jopus, causing Pam to rest her head upon his laps. He looked into her face and started telling her things.

"Verily I say unto you," uttered Jopus, "never shall thou thirst again."

"Really?" she said, smiling.

"You see, unlike all the other men you've known – or would have come to know had I not come into your life – I, having given you my water, now live in you. Always, always will I be in you. Indeed, I know that you have always craved me but my mission has ever put you off, for you had placed me upon a pedestal, concluding that I could never give you manly attention. So, I thought it wise that I should make it easier for you to get to know me, hence my coming here at the well today to find you. Besides, I know that your parents brought you to this place as an infant and abandoned you at the foot of the giant tree, following a prophesy that you would grow so beautiful that your own father would find you irresistibly attractive at pubescence and lose all his manly desire for your mother, his wife. The water you have given me today and that which I have given you were all part of that prophecy, and it has come to pass. Lucky are you because today you've received from me nothing but life itself," said Jopus with a dense air of reverence.

Amazed at Jopus manner and the details of her life he knew, she rose and took his hand, making him to rise too. She took him in a tight embrace, tears welling in her eyes.

"I love you," she said deeply affectionately.

"I love you too," responded Jopus equally affectionately, tightening his grip on her. Silence enveloped them. They heard each other's heart beat inside their chests.

Hardly had they disengaged when Jopus' friends appeared on the scene. All the twelve young missionaries were quizzical on their faces, but each kept everything to himself. Jopus with a woman! It was a marvel.

When Pam had left Jopus' presence and gone some meters away, one of them asked Jopus if Jopus did not crave anything to eat; to which Jopus responded robustly that his friends had no idea how great his food was, that it was not anything like the snacks they had gone to look for. They all looked at him, their silence speaking louder than words. Of course, this was not the first time Jopus was losing them in sophisticated philosophy. They did not pursue the matter any further.

Pam, who was now quite some distance from the scene, without her pail, was singing contentedly:

Like the woman at the well I was seeking
For things that could not satisfy
And then I heard my saviour speaking
Come to my well that never shall run dry

She got to Kakoth shopping centre. From one person to the next she went and told of this man, Jopus; this man who had told her of the ancient prophecy concerning her life, who possessed accurate knowledge about each of the men she had known and why they never could have met her needs; a man who had given her the kind of water that satisfied her once and for all.

So the people of Kakoth came to the well. Men and women they came to Jopus and his friends at the well. They longed to see and hear from this man of whom Pam had spoken in such glowing terms.

Jopus, a man with the gift of the garb, did not fail his listeners, these people of Kakoth. Using Pam's yellow pail that was half-full of water, Jopus sought to deliver a lasting lesson. He called up one son of Kakoth. He gave him the pail by the metallic handle. The people watched in silent concentration there near the well. Those at the edge of the crowd craned their necks forward so that they may get to see for themselves. Who knows but Jopus could well have been after a miracle.

"Is this pail half full or half empty? Give a reason for your answer," Jopus said to the young man.

"It depends," the young man replied.

"Come on," urged Jopus.

"Yeah. I do not know whether it was being filled or being emptied."

"That is not part of the question. Answer the question as asked."

"I am an optimist, if that is what you want to know. I have heard of this kind of thing many times before."

"Entering the Kingdom will be hard for those who feel they know a lot," said Jopus, actually grunting in obvious disappointment but going on with the pre-conceived lesson, a lesson on the need always to think good and hope-building thoughts, that even amidst want, such as was afflicting the people of Kakoth, there needed to be song and chants of joy, the need to rejoice.

Jopus went on to tell the people of Kakoth that he had the power to cause women who found it difficult to conceive to do so, to cause the dumb to speak and to cause the stupid to be smart. He asked the people of Kakoth to look forward to his second coming to the well, when he would work a number of these miracles.

And when they had seen him and heard his wisdom, wisdom spoken so eloquently, first in the language of the people of Kakoth and then in the language of literacy, each sentence being pure poetry, intoned most sweetly, they went back to their shops and stalls and homes, marvelling all the more, telling those who had not been there that Jopus was a great man.

Jopus and his friends trekked on to the headquarters of Jopus Holy Mission (JHM) to rest and plan for the sake of new territories in need of similar revival.

They got there. They were very tired, but the day was not done. Robo had a matter he needed settled. He followed

Jopus into his office, taking a seat in front of Jopus' mahogany desk.

"Yes, friend," invited Jopus, using that general but affectionate reference.

"Tell me, Holy Master," said Robo, leaning towards him as if conspiratorially."

"Yes."

"You have always taught us to keep off women as long as we are in this mission; to aspire to your standards of celibacy."

"Well, that is correct."

"I should fear to ask this, but then again you have ever encouraged us always to seek answers to whatever."

"Robo, you have never warned me whenever you have had any question for me."

"You are right. I have never had cause to raise questions along these lines."

"What exactly is it, Robo?"

"That woman – at the well."

"Which woman? There were many women at the well."

"Jopus!" called Robo, the first time he was addressing him by name, always having referred to him as Holy Master, since Jopus had called him to the Mission a decade before. Jopus had promised him that there lay fulfillment in the Mission such as no worldly pleasure could match; that women, fundamentally, were a distraction to commitment to the Mission, that if they were as he was, then he exhorted them to a celibate life.

"With how many people have you discussed me?"

"I never discuss people but matters."

"Don't you try to be clever with me, Robo," Jopus snapped, banging the table, his forehead creased with frowns. White saliva appeared at both corners of his mouth. He felt as though his friends had besieged him like an army; that they were knocking down the edifice of holiness he had erected around himself all his life. He recalled his taking wine secretly, and the young boy he had once pressed to his chest in this very office. His friends had all gone out to the field on mission. Robo's sitting there, looking at him so accusingly, was breaking him with tension and guilt.

"You have betrayed my faith in you and in JHM. This is the last time you and I are associating so."

"Robo!"

"But I shall carry on the Mission, which is greater than any one of us," said Robo as he rose. He left, closing the door behind himself.

That was how JHM split. The break-away Mission, Robo Holier Mission (RHM), took away three of the followers of Jopus.

Six

Uncle Manu

Joy Beatrice had always believed that Namwel Manu was her uncle. Now, a couple of days since her admission to St. Anne's Girls, a girl arrived to add to their number in the Form One class.

"Your sister!" exclaimed her neighbour, Nancy, as the new girl walked in, accompanied by the head girl. Nancy repeated those words under her breath, now adding, "You didn't tell me your sister too would come here."

Joy Beatrice could not find anything to say to herself, let alone to Nancy, who seemed more than sure that the new girl was her sister and that she had known she would join St. Anne's Girls. For moments that followed, Joy Beatrice kept stealing glances, even staring at the new girl.

Then a teacher walked in, a green-cover book entitled 'Excelling in English' held proudly to his chest. His entry somewhat eased the strange feeling that had now settled somewhere down in Joy Beatrice's stomach.

Mr. Ngatia asked the class to do self-introduction, instructing that from the first row backwards, they should quote their full name and a storybook that they had read.

"My name is Joy Beatrice Manu. I have read 'Njogu the Prophet'," Joy Beatrice said when her turn came. Her voice betrayed no strange emotion.

Others took their turn too, everyone getting it right. They indeed were here on merit. The new girl introduced herself. She said she was Anne Treeza Manu and that she had read 'The Bell Ringer'.

The lesson went on. They learnt about parts of speech, Mr. Ngatia delivering explanations so admirably. Joy Beatrice liked his handwriting too.

Now the bell rang to mark the beginning of lunch break. The class emptied but in no great haste. Joy Beatrice kept casting glances the new girl's way.

Nearly everyone had left the classroom. Joy Beatrice plucked up courage and started towards the new girl. She noticed that Joy Beatrice was coming to her. She rose. Joy Beatrice got to her. She opened up her arms for Joy Beatrice. They hugged, not fully understanding why they were doing this, and so naturally.

So was this Joy Beatrice's sister? They resembled so much. Their voices were so similar. They shared the name Manu. But, wondered Joy Beatrice, how come Anne Treeza did not know that she had an uncle by the name Namwel Manu? Namwel Manu, she told Anne Treeza, was the man who had brought her up. He had explained to her that his brother Norman Manu and wife had both passed away while she, their daughter, was still a toddler. It was natural therefore, he said, that he should take her in and be to her no less than a father. And, indeed, he had brought her up perfectly. A girl could never ask for more.

Later that evening, she and Anne Treeza went to the headmistress. They explained to her their strange state of circumstances. She understood them and empathized. She advised that Anne Treeza should take Joy Beatrice home. She gave them money for their fare to and from home.

John Manu, and not some dead Norman Manu, was the man who had sired Joy Beatrice. He had lost her, his first-born child, to a kidnapper. This whole state of affairs here at home brought Joy Beatrice such sad happiness.

The following day, their father accompanied them to school. He got to meet their kind headmistress. She promised him that she would make sure that Joy Beatrice goes through that drastic change in her life without it hurting her studies or social life.

Weeks came and went. It was now a school visiting day. Namwel Manu was among the first of parents and guardians to arrive in St. Anne's Girls that Saturday. Joy Beatrice spotted him and rushed to the headmistress to notify her of his presence. Mrs Hull advised her to be totally relaxed about everything. She told her just to meet Namwel Manu as if he were her uncle.

So Joy Beatrice was now with Namwel Manu at a tent that had been pitched in the open ground in the compound for purposes of this visiting day. She gave him a summary of how everything had been the past six weeks, everything except the big story. She effectively contained the hurt and tension that she felt to be talking to a man who had lied to her about her identity. At certain points in the course of the conversation, her face twitched quite a bit with bitterness, but she did well in keeping composed.

"Promise me your report form is going to make me even more proud of you when you come for Term One break," said Namwel Manu, looking into Joy Beatrice's eyes.

"I'll do well," she answered, looking aside.

"You promise?"

"I promise I shall do well," she said now looking him in the face, giving him something close to the assurance he required.

Namwel Manu then gave her pocket money – quite a tidy sum. She thanked him. He noticed tears welling up in her eyes as she did so.

"Anything the matter, Joy Beatrice?"

"Nothing. I – I simply am very much thankful for this," she said, managing a smile meant to keep her emotions at bay. Mrs Hull had asked her to handle everything as if everything else were normal; she was not going to let her down by breaking down.

"It's all right, Joy Beatrice. A bright girl such as you deserves the very best, isn't that so?" said Namwel Manu, ready to rise.

"Thanks a lot. I'm glad," she said.

"Now let me go and see your headmistress briefly before I leave."

"Okay," she said with a smile. She did not hug him. He took note of this but decided that it was part of expected changes that come with growing up.

Namwel Manu went over to the headmistress' office. She welcomed him and showed him to a seat.

"Joy Beatrice's father?"

"Her uncle. Oh, so you remember me."

"Of course I do, Mr Manu."

"Wow!"

"So, what do you do for a living?"

"I run my own business in Stone City."

"All right. That is great. Er…Joy Beatrice is a very good girl. You certainly are a very good uncle to her."

"Thank you. She deserves no less."

"That is one very promising girl, Mr Manu."

"That is for sure. I have great expectations of her."

"Any other great one you are bringing us soon?"

"Well, not very soon. My little girl is yet in Grade Three."

"All right, Mr Manu. So – you have a business card?"

"Oh yes. Let me give you one."

"Yes. Just in case of anything…you know, even business-wise."

"Certainly. Here is one for you."

"Thanks, Mr. Manu. It is a pleasure meeting you."

"Pleasure. I just came to say hello. I've seen the girl and now I wish to leave the capital to go and take care of other things."

"Of course."

"Let the good girl stay so."

"Okay. Good bye, Mr. Manu."

"Good bye."

About an hour later, Joy Beatrice's dad and mum arrived in St. Anne's Girls. While the lady carried a basket in her hand, the man had but the newspaper of day. In the basket were three hotpots, fixed one on top of another. They contained fried pieces of chicken, chapatti and soup respectively. The two were received by their two daughters, who then conducted them to the tent, at a corner.

Now there they were. They conversed. The girls told their parents about their academic progress as well as a number of things they needed, wanted or desired, and even those that bored and pissed them off. The parents updated their daughters on happenings at home, including how their little brother, Alex, was doing. The midday sun fell upon the multi-storey buildings that were the classrooms and dormitories of this magnificent national school, and upon its cute playgrounds, hexagon-shaped patterns of its paved paths, and all.

Anne Treeza was then sent to go and see if the headmistress was in her office and if so notify her that her father and mother wished to say hello to her. She rose, touched her green skirt here and there, and started for the centrally situated administration block. Her parents gave her a look from behind. Her body looked good. St. Anne's Girls was feeding her well.

In the meantime, Joy Beatrice told her parents that Namwel Manu had already visited her and left. As she reported this, tears welled up in her eyes the way they had done upon her receiving pocket money from Namwel a while before. She fought back the tears. Her parents noticed her emotional struggle.

Anne Treeza was now running back to them from the headmistress' office. John Manu turned his head to Joy Beatrice and told her to be happy. Anne Treeza reported that the headmistress had said they could go and see her right then.

So John Manu led his wife to the office where he had been, about six weeks earlier. The girls remained behind to have a good time, thanks to the basket their mum had carried with her.

Having washed their hands with water from a bottle, they uncovered the hotpots. Each picked a chicken thigh. Their teeth sank simultaneously into the flesh of the pieces; and on chewing what they had bitten, their unspoken verdict was that their mother was the best cook in the whole world. But then again, looking at every other girl seated on some cloth spread on the ground around there, with hotpots near them, you got the idea that every one of them thought her mother the very best.

In the headmistress' office, John Manu and wife, seated opposite each other in front of Mrs Hull, talked about their daughters regarding academic matters. All the while, however, each knew that the Uncle Manu issue was what they were preparing themselves to talk about.

"Now, Mr. Manu," began the headmistress, "earlier on today I was addressing another Mr Manu, but who is not even your relative!"

"And who has all the while lied to my daughter that he was my brother," said John Manu.

"You know, I had wondered how come he and you share a surname. Anyway, what I would like to share with the two of you is that I have seen a lot of things in my long career. Let me tell you that in a case such as this one, a lot of care needs to be taken. Of course, you now have your daughter back, but that man, as far as he is concerned, is still her uncle and guardian. He was here, not long ago, seated right where you are, Mrs Manu. He even has big dreams for the girl. In short, you have to be careful; so that when he is finally made to realize that all he has done and is doing is wrong, no one will be at risk. Mr Manu, you told me your daughter was kidnapped, right?"

"Yes."

"Yes, that makes him a criminal – all right we are yet to find out exactly how he got her, but whatever it is, it is wrong to keep a child that is not yours, without even seeming to be bothered."

"That is right."

"Now, I have his contact and other details. As I suggested to you the other day, this is no less than a police case. It is going to be a court case."

"Of course."

"He may even seek to harm you or the girl once you take her from him, you know?"

"That is absolutely true."

"Court?" Norman Manu's wife interjected.

"Once it is a police case, it ends up in court," responded her husband.

"I don't like courts."

"You speak like a woman indeed, Tabitha. This is not a light matter," protested Norman Manu.

"Mr. Manu, you forget that I am a woman."

"No, no, no. By all means you... you are one of the most sensible people I have ever met."

"It's all right, Mr Manu."

"Okay, as I was saying, you are absolutely right, Mrs Hull. The man may react in a damaging way upon our taking back the girl from him. He has to be put behind bars."

"We have our daughter back, John. She is not going back to that man. God will protect her," said the wife.

"Once a kidnapper, always a kidnapper! We cannot be as naïve as you want us to be, Tabitha."

"It's all right, Mr and Mrs Manu," intercepted the headmistress. "All I know is that I have a solemn responsibility towards the girl, and I shall do whatever I can to ensure she lives to be the person she wants to be. Everything will turn out just fine."

"Thank you," said the parents in unison.

"Anne Treeza is not only bright but she is also an excellent athlete."

"She takes after her mother," said Mrs Manu, smiling.

"In athletics, yes," said her husband.

"Mr. Manu, so you admit to not being particularly athletic, huh?" said Mrs Hull.

"No doubt I can beat a lot of people in a race," said John Manu. They laughed together.

The parents of Joy Beatrice and Anne Treza left St. Anne's Girls for home. Mrs Hull had told them that she would think of a way forward and give them a call. They drove home. For the first time the two were finding it easier to talk about their situation. They had of late been very damp of spirit. The visit indeed had achieved much more than just going to see children at school.

A week to the end of Term One, Mrs Hull called the Manus on the phone, asking them to come to St. Anne's Girls to meet Namwel Manu. She had had a very long telephone conversation with Namwel Manu, during which she prepared him for the said meeting. Namwel Manu had first been in denial, but Mrs Hull had expertly released to him one fact after another, and there certainly had been no way out for him but to face those facts. The girl had her own parents, alive and well.

The D-day came. It was inside the same office of the headmistress. The parents of Joy Beatrice were there seated. The man who had made her believe that he was her uncle was there too. They had come to find a solution, together.

Hardly had Mrs. Hull made a sentence of welcome when a large tear drop fell onto the breast of Namwel Manu's coat. Another one did the same. Emotion began to choke him.

Soon his tears were flowing with surprising copiousness, his head shaking, the lump he felt in his throat seeming to gain in size. Mrs Hull rose and closed the door so that no commotion should result from the man's crying inside her office.

Namwel Manu now held his head, his elbows supported upon his thighs, so that he faced the floor. He kept shaking his head in that position. The exchange that he and his wife had had two nights before now flooded his mind. It was upon that night that he had disclosed to his wife his decade-old deed, five years after he had decided to marry again. He had disclosed to her and their little daughter that when his first wife died heavy with pregnancy, he had gone into a near-depression; that when he had recovered, he had made a decision not to marry but adopt a child. As he was driving from the capital that particular evening, he had noticed a child alone by the road. He had grabbed her into the car and driven off. "I am your uncle; we are going to live in a very good place," he had said to the child as he accelerated to Stone City. He had then crafted lies which he would tell to whomever raised any questions.

Oh, this moment was breaking him, here in Mrs Hull's office. The other three stared blankly in the air, waiting for Namwel Manu to calm down. John Manu's gaze wandered about, from wall to wall. He saw a certificate that had the name Anne Treeza Manu inscribed calligraphically on it.

Namwel Manu now raised his head. He was a fake uncle. He was a kidnapper. Oh God! His lips trembled as he cleared his throat, determined to say something, this thing that had choked him so much.

"I'm sorry for my dark deeds. Forgive me. They are too horrible for me to repeat. Just find it in your heart that you should forgive me," Namwel Manu said, his eyes resting briefly on the mother and then father of the girl he had lived with for ten solid years.

John Manu rose from his seat. He took Namwel Manu in embrace. The two seated women looked at the two hugging men. Tears dropped from the face of the girl's mother.

The two men disengaged. Mrs Hull cleared her throat and said, "It's done. Let us drive to the CBD and have a cup of tea together with the girls."

Later, at about five o'clock that evening, smiling faces emerged from Hotel Magenta. Joy Beatrice held hands with the mother and her sister Anne Treeza. Their father walked on the other side of their mother. Mrs Hull was by Namwel Namu's side, walking towards his car. The girls would say good bye to their parents and then be driven back to school in their headmistress' car. Joy Beatrice felt a unique sense of freedom in her heart. She swore to herself that she would work hard and become a writer to tell the story of her life, as well as those of the lives of others.

Seven

Origin of Birth

When the rulers of Polo, the land far beyond the clouds, had made the first man and the first woman, there was a general acknowledgement among these rulers that the two beings they had made were great. As a matter of fact, they were shocked that their creative effort had yielded an outcome that was beyond the wildest of their expectations. Their constant glances at Man and Woman confirmed this; and, certainly, they would have turned down any suggestion from any quarters that they should try to create anything finer than Man and Woman.

And as time went by, season giving way to season, Man and Woman greatly gained in physical attractiveness. Woman blossomed into an utterly irresistible being. Man developed into such a hunk. The two became a point of greater and greater fascination in the eyes of those who had made them, the twenty-four rulers of Polo.

It had taken the rulers a great deal of careful thinking, planning and imagination as they put together parts that were to constitute the created living individuals and, as we already have seen, the outcome was truly fine. Now, more than twenty-three seasons since the individuals were made, it could not escape notice that the two certainly were more than just fine creatures.

While their makers moulded them from holy clay those twenty-three seasons past, none of them, in all their omniscience, had any idea what the full extent of Man and Woman's capacity would be. Now they were coming alive to this great capacity of Man and Woman. That the two were so great was perhaps no more obvious than it was in the way they walked about in Polo. Their calm confidence and serenity elicited in the rulers something of a cautious fascination. The created beings existed in absolute bliss. Not a single worry had they; not a single duty. Theirs was to enjoy the beauty of existence, and only this was what they did there in Polo, the land beyond the clouds. They were by each other's side all the time. They held hands as they watched nature. One would be pointing to the other this or that breathtaking thing in their already perfect environment. Often they would stop and stand close so as to listen to each other's explanation or description of this or that observation made. Man particularly often outdid himself in describing nature. For instance, during one of their now habitual morning strolls around Polo, Man had amazed Woman by rushing to a certain lovely flower and, laying the back of his hand upon its petals, said, facing Woman:

> "None of the rulers knows
> That here this morning glory grows
> To please the senses of the sensitive
> And weave afresh the creation narrative."

And the excellence of Man's voice fixed the music of those words deep inside Woman's heart. She remained rooted to the spot, seeming transfixed, looking at him with a profound sense of appreciation.

Man then returned to her, took her hand and they walked on, surveying the beauty of Polo, the land beyond the clouds.

It was that compact closeness of the two created beings that some two Polo rulers now stopped to marvel at. It was early afternoon and Man and Woman were seated closely under a pawpaw tree.

"They are awesome, aren't they?" commented Koth, the Polo ruler in charge of rainmaking.

"Indeed!" responded Kodhi, his counterpart in charge of new life.

The two rulers had just met where the paths from their private abodes crossed on their way to The Pantheon, their meeting place.

And at the meeting place, Koth and Kodhi, who were among the last to arrive, realized that it was the general feeling among the rulers that Man and Woman needed to be discussed seriously. Informal comments before the debate proper indicated the existence of real anxiety among the rulers as to the future of Man and Woman in Polo, the land above the clouds.

So, Man and Woman became the afternoon's sole agenda. The Pantheon had to debate the matter exhaustively and reach a decision that would satisfy standards of divine sagacity and at the same time meet the rulers' pragmatic expectations.

From their contributions to the debate, it was absolutely clear that Polo was not at ease. Speaker after speaker communicated, with divine eloquence, the fact that they felt and feared that if something was not done to make the created beings a little lower, it was just a matter of time before Man and Woman acted to establish themselves as superior and supreme in Polo, the land beyond the clouds.

So now it was Kodhi's time to contribute to the wonderfully moderated debate in The Pantheon, presided over this afternoon by Muya, the Polo ruler in charge of gas-making. Kodhi explained to a very attentive House that when he designed Woman's birth structures which were then placed inside the moulding that was to become the individual known as Woman, he had done so in such a way that between nine and twelve seasons after creation, Woman would have developed the capacity to generate a new being. That would occur, he added, the moment Woman and Man would make love.

Kodhi reminded the rulers of some little disc that he had asked to be allowed to insert in the brains of Man and Woman, at the mention of which they all nodded. It had been after quite some argument that the insertion of the disc had been allowed. Kodhi had had to plead that he be trusted as the ruler in charge of life; that his fellow rulers just had to take his word that the disc in question was absolutely necessary even if he may not afford to explain it to his fellow creators as clearly as they expected each other to do at every step in the process of moulding Man and Woman from holy clay.

The disc, Kodhi revealed, was what had shut Man's and Woman's sexual curiosity thus far, so that even though Man and Woman went about naked, and the well-formed breasts and bum of Woman were always in full view, Man felt no arousal; and also even though Man's tools of life hung down there, dangling about lazily, it was not possible for Woman to desire Man in that intimate way.

Kodhi concluded his contribution by asking The Pantheon to decide there and then whether the disc in Man's and Woman's brains should be removed.

Le, the Polo ruler in charge of wild animals, rose on a point of order. He sought direction from the chair as to what the disc and sexual curiosity had to do with the chief concern of Polo at that particular moment: what to do to prevent Man and Woman from acting to establish themselves as superior and supreme in Polo.

Kodhi returned to the floor and expounded thus: "My dear, Le, and The Pantheon at large, we must be able to understand certain fundamental things about existence. Fellow rulers, we are in control because of our capacity to create. In such admirable cooperation we made all that is – the finest of which, I dare say, were Man and Woman. And as is now abundantly clear, these two turned out to be of great capacity, the full extent of which, frankly speaking, we never imagined as we formed them from holy clay. My point, fellow rulers, is that should it dawn on these two that they too can bring forth beings of their own nature, it is without a doubt that they shall deem themselves our equals and this will be the beginning of a painful battle for superiority between them and us."

Kodhi resumed his seat after that lucid delivery.

Chieng, one of the most profound philosophers of the Polo rulers, now had the floor. He started by recognizing Kodhi's great wisdom and foresight with regard to the matter of the disc. He caused laughter by saying that he had trusted Kodhi, on the creation day, concerning the disc insertion. (What was amusing was that it was he himself who had made a rather strong statement on the creation day: that whatever someone could not explain clearly did not deserve the benefit of the doubt.)

Chieng moved on to observe that had it not been for Kodhi's wisdom during creation, Polo would suddenly have been faced with a crisis in which the created would also create in the land of creation. He added that they, as rulers of Polo, owed Kodhi much gratitude for having come up with the disc.

Chieng resumed his seat. But although he had spoken quite well, he had not offered any solution as to the pressing matter: what exactly was to be done to prevent Man and Woman from acting to establish themselves as superior and supreme in Polo, that land beyond the clouds.

The presiding chairperson, Muya, the ruler in charge of gas-making, raised his head and cast a sweeping glance in The Pantheon for any indication of a ready contribution, but no one seemed to have anything to say about the situation that was now almost portraying Polo rulers as not-all-that-wise after all.

The meeting came to an end. The rulers left The Pantheon for their private abodes. Each was now even more worried about what Man and Woman could suddenly do in Polo, given their amazing intelligence and their care-free kind of life there in the land beyond the clouds.

On their way back to their private abodes, Koth and Kodhi again saw Man and Woman. This time round the two created beings were seated upon a rock. Their heads were brought so close together. Apparently, they were in some deep conversation. The two rulers' suspicions intensified. What was to be done to Man and Woman remained the question.

The two rulers went their different ways when they got to where the paths to their private abodes diverged. Little would be their sleep that night.

The following day, all twenty-four rulers of Polo converged in The Pantheon much earlier than usual. Of course, they had not planned, at the end of the previous meeting, that such should be the case; however, here they all were now, so early this afternoon. This, no doubt, bespoke the seriousness with which they were all treating the question as to what they should do with Man and Woman so as to nip in the bud any possible ambitions of theirs to take over the leadership of Polo. In a word, how to deal with Man and Woman still remained the question that The Pantheon had to answer.

Debate resumed. Muya still presided as chairperson, for he had performed very well in guiding debate on this particular matter, allowing members to express their opinions freely and fully and at the same time ensuring that contributions were focused.

Fortunately for them, today they never had to argue much. The matter was already very well understood. What members wanted to hear today was something of a way forward.

After a couple of contributions, in which no real solution could be discerned, Chieng took the floor. He seemed to have a solution, for his forehead wrinkled with seriousness.

"Tough situations call for tough decisions," said the profound philosopher. He went on: "Radical as my proposal is – for I cannot pretend that it's not – it is the only solution. Fellow rulers, Man and Woman must be relocated to the land of Kakoth, the land far below the clouds."

And with that concise piece of contribution, Chieng resumed his seat.

And no sooner had Chieng resumed his seat than Koth rose to his feet. Koth declared full support for Chieng's proposal, telling The Pantheon that although he had nothing against Man and Woman staying in Polo, his instincts told him that trouble was in the offing if things remained the way they were. He said that they had a responsibility as rulers of Polo to do anything and everything in their power to forestall any form of trouble there in the land beyond the clouds.

Koth added pithily that it was better to err on the side of caution. He earned himself spontaneous claps for this. He concluded humorously that he wished Man and Woman all the best in the land far below the clouds, and that he would dutifully give them rain as and when they would need it.

A few more contributions were heard, nearly all of which were in support of Chieng's proposal that Man and Woman be relocated to the land far below the clouds. The sole dissenting voice was that of Lowo, the ruler in charge of land. Lowo asked The Pantheon whether it made any sense that they, being creators and rulers, should fear mere created beings. He criticized his fellow rulers for lack of confidence in their ability to handle Man and Woman, mere created beings. He said that it would be truly irresponsible of them if they should send to exile the wonderful beings whom they had laboured so much to make, and just on account of unfounded fear and suspicion that the created beings could one day seek take over the leadership of Polo. Lowo caused laughter when he angrily demanded that Chieng tell The Pantheon who it was that had told him that Man and Woman wanted to take over the leadership of Polo.

So, Lowo, the absolute minority, had his say while the majority had their way. It was resolved that in the interest of stability and proper running of the affairs of Polo, and in the interest of the freedom of Man and Woman, the proposed relocation be effected.

Kodhi was asked to go and surgically remove from Man's and Woman's brains the disc that he had inserted there during creation for the purpose of inhibiting their sexual curiosity. As Kodhi did this, he was to explain to Man and Woman that they were thereby being given the golden gift of birth. He was to persuade them that the beauty of birth while they lived in the land below the clouds would be infinitely greater than their residing in Polo with the disc that had so far kept them from desiring each other.

Later, as Kodhi performed surgical operations simultaneously on Man and Woman, moving with his surgical blade from one to the other and then back, desire steadily grew inside the two created beings. And as the disc was almost being dislodged, desire intensified in them. And Kodhi kept talking persuasively about Man and Woman's planned life down in the land below the clouds as he took the surgical procedure towards its successful end. And Man and Woman liked what was happening in their bodies, the wave of desire spreading like current throughout their systems. They as well fell in love with the promise fed into their ears by Kodhi's sweet persuasion, the promise that this great desire would abide in them always in the land far below the clouds; that this feeling would be wholly theirs if only they left Polo.

So, twenty-four seasons since the rulers of Polo had made Man and Woman, the two created beings landed in Kakoth, the land far below the clouds.

And they dwelt in the land far below the clouds, so far away from where they had been made, their original home.

And there they had many children and were happy about the whole arrangement.

The children that Man and Woman got began to feel sexual desire much early in their life; for they had been born without the disc that blocked this desire. And their parents had a rough time making sure that the powerful desire never controlled their actions while they were yet so young. Their parents had to remind them constantly that exercising self-control was necessary, for they had first to acquire life skills before engaging in the gift of birth, that golden gift given to their first grandparents. Female grandchildren of Woman were advised never to sit *angewa*, with legs parted, for this would instantly cause a flood of desire in any male grandchild of Woman, as everyone in the land of Kakoth was born without the disc that blocked desire.

And these children's children were like their parents, born without the disc that blocked desire. And it all went on and on, and is the case even today. And the rulers of Polo have stuck to that decision of theirs, made so long ago in The Pantheon, the decision that created beings should have their freedom and manage it according to their own will in the land below the clouds. And like their forebears, children of created beings remain reluctant to give up their desire even in exchange for life in Polo, the land beyond the clouds. They just cannot imagine life without birth.

That is how it happened so long ago. May I grow as tall as the tree at my uncle's home.

Eight

Origin of Prostitution

L ong ago, in the land of Kakoth, the land far below the clouds, there lived a girl known popularly as Atoti daughter of Kakoth. Needless to say, Atoti was not the only daughter of this land, but, as it is in life, a given place or generation often has a certain individual who turns out to be the most prominent or notorious in the living memory. Such was the case with Atoti daughter of Kakoth.

Atoti daughter of Kakoth was a ninth-generation grandchild of the first human beings, Man and Woman. Born and brought up in coastal Kakoth, this girl was to have far-reaching influence on the lives of members of her generation and future ones. As a matter of fact, the rulers of Polo, the land far beyond the clouds, gasped at the uncanny deeds of Atoti daughter of Kakoth, this maiden whose beauty and charm is a great story for another day.

Now, Atoti daughter of Kakoth sometimes decided to disturb the existing order, simply to see what the consequences would be. Well, maybe this needed not be very much surprising, for, quite often, this happened where exquisitely beautiful people were concerned. Indeed, with regard to Kakoth, it needed not be surprising at all. Daughters of this land were liberally granted the fairness of face. The sons too were quite well endowed, being tall, dark and not bad-looking either. Given this reality, the people of Kakoth tended to have a rather dismissive attitude towards anyone whom they perceived to fall outside the brackets of good looks. As a result, any *raracha*, one not well blessed with looks, for instance would easily lose out on any competitive thing – be it selecting those who were to offer company, an appointment, an election, granting of a chance for a conversation and so on. A *jaber*, one endowed with looks, on the other hand, easily found favour in the eyes of the people. Such a one naturally was considered innocent, good, smart, and so on; and only when they had proved otherwise would minds change about them – and even then there still would be some trace of trust for them, some psychological support for, and solidarity with, them. This, perhaps, was why the likes of Atoti daughter of Kakoth felt that they were entitled to quite some freedom to venture into the bad side of life and, as well, to come out of it unscathed, if possible.

This generation, the ninth generation of the people of Kakoth, was generally troublesome. Atoti daughter of Kakoth only outdid herself in all this, but the whole generation was a difficult one. Since the days of Man and Woman, the first parents of Kakoth children had been managed with an admirable degree of ease and success. But things had now changed, and they had changed utterly. Without the disc that blocked desire, which had been inserted in the brains of Man and Woman but later removed following a resolution by rulers of Polo, human beings certainly were to experience difficulty in keeping their self-control and social order. But norms, expressed in the language and deeds of the people of Kakoth, had done very well in keeping order in the land, the land below the clouds. For generations all was well. The ninth generation, however, certainly was queer. Children challenged norms and came up with very wild suggestions and proposals. Atoti daughter of Kakoth, she of great beauty and charm, was at the forefront of this ninth generation's queerness.

As it was, coastal Kakoth, where Atoti daughter of Kakoth was born and brought up, was a place of fruits, the most dominant of these being coconut, the trees of which grew very tall, as if threatening to reach Polo, the land above the clouds.

Now until this girl, Atoti daughter of Kakoth, no daughter of Kakoth had ever dared to violate the unwritten Kakoth rule that a girl should never climb a coconut tree. Many were the generations that had been born since the first parents, Man and Woman, but rules, especially those taken as seriously as this one about the coconut tree, were never even debated, let alone violated.

But Atoti daughter of Kakoth had watched the way boys twined the tall stems of the coconut trees, on their way to the top, to pluck their precious fruits, and now she decided that she was going to do what the boys were doing, and even better.

To climb a coconut tree in coastal Kakoth, one first hugged the stem tightly, the arms twining around it. The legs, down there, also held the stem in a similar manner, twining around it. Then one would launch oneself up the stem by freeing up one's arms and getting them to hold a higher portion of the stem, holding it tightly there. Almost simultaneously, one released the grip of one's legs twined down there round the stem, drew the whole lower portion of the body up the stem, hence creating a net movement up the coconut tree. Another such movement would be initiated, and another and another, up, up and up to top of the tall tree where the great fruits were.

So, Atoti daughter of Kakoth, in these late hours of the morning, when lunch was already cooking in many a coastal Kakoth home, was alone, here in the fields, determined to pluck coconut fruits for herself. Ordinarily, a father brought home the fruits, or instructed a son to scale a coconut tree in the homestead and pluck a specific number of the golden fruits, upon which occasions everyone in the family would rush to him to be given one. Atoti daughter of Kakoth was here to apply the coconut-climbing skills herself, skills which she had observed and learnt and was only yet to try out practically.

And there now she was, tightly hugging the coconut tree and twining her legs around it just as tightly. She released the grip of her legs on the stem so as to draw her lower body upwards. She succeeded in making the first net movement up the tree.

Atoti daughter of Kakoth again released the grip of her legs on the stem so as to draw her lower body upwards. She succeeded in making the second net movement up the tree. Her breathing started becoming heavy. She made the third, fourth and fifth movements in quick succession. She then held on so as to take some rest in the course of that long journey to the top, where the golden fruits were.

A boy happened to have come to the foot of the tree and was now studying this strange phenomenon of a daughter of Kakoth climbing a coconut tree. He watched her up there, making determined movements up the tree. He marvelled both at her audacity and capacity.

In the process, the boy saw her private parts. A wave of desire spread throughout his body. He looked up with even greater keenness, waiting for her to initiate another movement, whereupon she would free up her legs in readiness to draw her lower body up the stem, thereby exposing some more of what his eyes wanted so much down there.

Atoti daughter of Kakoth released the grip of her legs on the stem and drew her lower body upwards. The boy saw her private parts again, now like the flashing of lightning. He remained glued to the aerial scene, his neck staying craned at an uncomfortable but much needed angle for the next sight.

And he got aroused – completely so, wetting his pair of shorts with the product of that kind of desire.

Atoti daughter of Kakoth, oblivious of what was going on below her, scaled the tree some more, so determined to get to the top where the great fruits were.

And upon yet another sight of her private parts, the boy now yelled helplessly down there, unable to contain himself anymore. Atoti daughter of Kakoth had bewitched him.

Atoti cast a downward look. She realized that the boy had actually seen her nakedness, and this made her feel some sudden weakness throughout her body. Oh, she lost her grip on the tree and fell to the sandy ground below with a thud.

The boy went over to her where she lay, seeming as if she had passed out.

"Don't you touch me!" she protested when the boy tried to find out, with his hand, if she was all right. The boy cringed and retreated.

Then Atoti got to a seated position.

The boy looked at her face. Seeing that she was all right in spite of the fall, and, above all, recognizing her stunning looks, he went right ahead and told her that if she allowed him an intercourse, he would go up the tree and pluck coconuts for her.

Atoti daughter of Kakoth thought for a moment and decided that if that was all it would take for her to get what she had come here for, and which she had come so close to getting, she was going to give the boy what he had asked for.

"But first, climb and pluck the fruits for me," she said to him.

With the kind of eagerness that only a great promise could ever generate, the boy scaled the tall tree with such effortlessness that he made Atoti daughter of Kakoth say to herself that certain things simply were meant for boys. Within no time at all, he was atop the tall coconut tree, where the great fruits clustered invitingly.

And the boy plucked the fruits from that great height, releasing one after another to fall freely to the sandy ground. Then he climbed down.

And Atoti daughter of Kakoth delivered the promise she had made to him. They did the forbidden deed right there at the foot of the coconut tree, on the sandy ground.

Then the boy went his way, satisfied. Atoti daughter of Kakoth wrapped up her fruits in a waist cloth, these fruits that she had so much wanted. She carried them, and started for home.

How she managed to get the fruits, she decided on her way home, would form part of Kakoth tales: the girl who climbed a coconut tree. She would tell of how easily she climbed a coconut tree and actually plucked the great fruits.

Of course, her parents were furious. How could she go against the traditional rule of Kakoth that a girl should not climb a coconut tree?

Even though nothing that they said in their angry criticism of their daughter had exactly brought out the reason a girl should not climb a coconut tree, what was absolutely clear in all this was that the girl had broken a rule. She had broken a rule knowingly and, as such, had brought a curse on the entire land of Kakoth, the land below the clouds. But the beautiful and charming girl was not moved even one bit by this talk of a curse on the land. In fact to her she was a fearless pioneer, and this needed to be known throughout the land.

And from then on, whenever Atoti daughter of Kakoth would feel an urge for coconut, she would contact that boy, and at the coconut tree they would meet. The promise would now not even be spoken. The expert coconut tree climber would quickly do his duty and the beautiful and charming Atoti daughter of Kakoth would promptly pay him for it in that very manner that pleased him most.

As time went by, Atoti daughter of Kakoth reasoned within herself that what she possessed actually was an inexhaustible natural resource which needed to win her not only coconuts but also any other thing that she needed or desired. Rolling her eyes in the deepest contemplation she had ever indulged in, she thought that this was, and would remain, the greatest discovery ever in the land below the clouds.

So, using this same promise, she was soon getting showered with such things as beaded necklaces, trinkets, mother of pearl and all. Many other things she got, which she donned and proudly displayed.

And because Atoti daughter of Kakoth was already exquisitely fair, these accessories now almost turned her into a young goddess in the eyes of her people, some of whom even feared her because she got anything that she wanted in life – and when she wanted it.

And other daughters of Kakoth soon learnt this trade from her, and carried it out not just in coastal Kakoth but throughout the land. Like wild fire it spread all over. Those in the interior parts of the land of Kakoth listened with open mouths to the story of the possibility that they could get almost anything they wanted in such a simple way.

And as seasons passed, this trade, started by Atoti daughter of Kakoth, got perfected. It developed to sophisticated levels when the land of Kakoth started using a standard medium of exchange of goods and services. With that standard medium of exchange of goods and services, it was no longer necessary for a son of Kakoth to climb tall fruit trees literally. It was sufficient for him just to produce the standard medium of exchange after being pleased by a daughter of Kakoth, who would then go and buy herself whatever her heart desired.

So, what Atoti daughter of Kakoth had first done just so as to get herself some fruits had now changed into a fully-fledged formidable trade. About this trade parents and leaders of Kakoth made a lot of noise in condemnation, but the more the noise the more popular the trade became. Indeed, even those who made such noise were quietly amazed that such a trade should be possible. The wealthy ones in Kakoth indulged in it purely for pleasure. The poor and the average needed it to make ends meet and to have their needs better met.

Everyone soon understood that this was a unique kind of trade. It had the readiest and most permanent demand of all services on offer in the entire land of Kakoth, the land far below the clouds. Indeed, in some areas in the land of Kakoth, rules were made, now not prohibiting it but seeking to have those earning from it share the benefits with the rest of the people, especially those with little material possession.

And in Polo, the land above the clouds, Kodhi, the ruler in charge of new life, sometimes felt ashamed that he personally had removed from Man and Woman the disc that blocked desire. Given the state of circumstances in the land below the clouds, Kodhi remained ill at ease, ever feeling that things could have been handled differently in Polo before Man and Woman were made to leave to go and dwell in the land below the clouds.

And that is how things happened so long ago in the created land of Kakoth. May I grow as tall as the tree at my uncle's home.

Nine

The Third Sin

Christabelle saw me and made to slip into her parents' compound. I called her loudly, telling her that she was not going to succeed in her attempt to avoid me. And this stopped her. She stood, holding the frame of the wooden gate which she had already pushed open. She made a step backwards, drawing the gate closed in the process. I beckoned her forcefully. She started towards my direction, clearly hating having to do so. She knew what I wanted from her. At my parents' gate I waited for her, never taking my gaze off her.

So she and I now shook hands. I ushered her into my parents' compound, five doors from hers. The estate was quiet. The afternoon was hot. My parents were away at work.

The door creaked open. My little brother had heard the gate being opened and had rushed to unlock the door for us.

"What's up, bro?" I greeted Albert.

"What's up," he responded.

"Come on in," I said to Christabelle, motioning her into the living room.

"Hi, Albert," she said to my little brother.

"Hi," my little brother responded simply.

The three of us were now seated in the living room. An action movie was paused on the screen. (Clearly, Albert had been having a good afternoon.) A framed photo of my parents rested on the wall, and near this was a calendar with a large picture of a lioness and its cub standing by it trustfully.

Albert stopped the movie altogether. He said he was going to purchase some beef from the butchery for the evening's meal as had been instructed by Mother. I said it was all right.

I now fixed some juice for Christabelle and myself. Then we got talking. I desired to milk her dry concerning her school, Treasures High. I sought to get an insider's story as to why Treasures High had fallen from grace to grass. My school had beaten Treasures High two years previously but we had been shocked that we had been able to do that. We had not celebrated. Beating them for the second year running was what had caused celebration, wild celebration. Treasures High had always been an academic giant. To confirm that we had edged out this giant was just incredibly great for us. It would take time, quite some time, for it to sink in.

"So – Treasures. Christabelle, your mighty Treasures High – what happened?"

"I do not wish to be associated with what goes on at Treasures High," Christabelle said to me firmly.

"Oh, come on, Christabelle. You are part and parcel of Treasures High. You cannot just shrug off what happens there. Everyone in the estate sees you and thinks of Treasures High. You just cannot avoid it, Christabelle."

"Treasures High and I are two very different things, Francis."

"All the same, may I know what the matter really is inside there – I mean, there has to be something terribly wrong."

And Christabelle decided to tell all that she could, to satisfy my curiosity once and for all so that I could leave her alone from then on.

She revealed to me that the first time Treasures High had fared badly in national examinations, it was Christian Religious Education to blame. The teacher concerned had led the whole school community in passionate prayers, during which session she had spoken in tongues and nearly all the candidates had fallen to the ground under the influence of 'The Spirit'. Upon the eve of the Christian Religious Education examination, she had summoned her class at night for a further round of prayers. She had announced this at the assembly earlier in the day to make her intention clear and straight forward. She had declared at the assembly that hers was more than a subject; that it was God's word itself, and, as such, special power from above was needed if one was to face, tackle and be successful in an examination in the subject. And it was at that night session of prayers that she had given the candidates answers to examination questions, the examination that they would tackle the following day.

"Hence the notorious Mid-night Power Prayers?" I interjected amidst Christabelle's frank account.

"Yes," she said, nodding.

She went on: "As for last year, I think the school took too much time handling scandals."

"Scandals?"

"Yes. There was this teacher called Mr. Weche. He was a cool guy, you know. He trained us in drama. One evening after practice he released everybody except Betty, for whom he said he had a special word, given her star role, and which needed not delay everyone else.

No doubt, Betty was gorgeous. Mr Weche could only have resisted the temptation to get his hands onto those attractive thighs by divine supervision. So about drama he talked to Betty there, just the two of them in the drama and film room. Then he rose and moved towards her as he mumbled words of congratulations to her on a line she had just delivered as he desired it to be. As he addressed her, he undressed her in his mind. He pictured those fine breasts in the absence of the white blouse. They were fruits he felt like picking. He hugged her, her breasts pressing pleasantly upon his chest. He looked her in the face. His gaze rested on her lovely lips. He got his hands onto her hips, those hips that held her blue skirt so attractively, and which he daily desired. He brushed his lips against hers. He could feel her heart already beating fast. He unbuttoned her skirt and made it fall down to her legs. He raised her blouse, exposing white panties. What he saw greatly excited him. He kissed her more passionately on the lips. He began petting her heavily.

It was at that point that Rebecca, a classmate of Betty's, called out to Betty, who, she had been told, was receiving instructions in the drama and film room. Why she had come and called Betty only she could tell, for she walked away from the vicinity of the drama and film room just as she had walked there. But that action of hers counted for something significant. It brought to a stop what was going on inside. Betty drew up her skirt and did it up. Mr Weche, struggling to keep his manhood down, uttered confused instructions just so as to diffuse the un-dramatic silence in the room. He then, in a most agent voice, asked that whoever was calling should give Betty just a moment to repeat a few lines which she was perfecting.

And, as one would expect, the matter spread to scandalous proportions within no time. It was only with a friend, one friend she trusted was not the gossipy type, that Betty had shared the happenings of that evening. Either this friend or the proverbial walls that have ears had spread this matter, Betty said to herself the following day when giggles were directed towards her wherever she turned."

At that point Christabelle served more juice into her glass. In the silent interlude I regarded Christabelle with a mixture of desire and awe. She was such a good narrator. Her language was excellent, and this, I thought to myself, demonstrated that Treasures High was a great school to learn in after all. I enquired if the matter had been pursued further, if any action had been taken against the sinners. Christabelle answered that Mr Weche had been questioned on the matter but had denied any involvement in any act of indecency, adding that such were but absurd allegations levelled against him by jealous enemies of his success in drama. And Betty herself was said to have been bribed by Mr Weche into giving the matter a wide berth. Christabelle added that the matter would be raised from time to time, but then it would be suppressed each time, although eventually Mr Weche got a transfer from Treasures High.

Just as Christabelle started on the third sin at Treasures High, I realized that I could not contain myself. The story she had just told me so nicely now made me imagine myself the man called Mr Weche, and Christabelle the gorgeous girl that she called Betty. I had loved the narration very much but I now wanted the lovely narrator herself. My desire for her was now overwhelming.

So when the gate opened and then shut loudly, I felt like a bull driven to heat but then denied an equally ready cow. It was my mother, returning from work. Christabelle, who, as far as I could judge, had the same feelings I had, looked to me disappointed too. Christabelle made to get to the third sin at Treasures High with clarity, but she was now hardly coherent. I sensed that she might not have had a third story after all, that the third sin ought to have taken place right here in my parents' living room if my mother had not returned at the time she did, which was much earlier than usual.

And Christabelle rose and begged to leave. I granted her leave. She said bye to my mother.

And when Christabelle had just left, my mother talked to me against a sin that Christabelle and I had never committed, but which she had a strong impression we had. I said to her that she was wrong to be thinking whatever she was thinking about me and Christabelle. She said that she was not saying that Christabelle and I had actually done anything, but that she knew people who had committed a sin when she looked at their faces. This contradiction in Mother's statement made me feel and decide that it was useless talking to her. How could she begin saying that she was not saying we had done anything, only to add, almost directly, that we had done it and that it was obvious on our faces?

And as my mother and I tussled psychologically over what she was convinced had happened, and which could have happened anyway but for her arrival, my little brother got back from the shopping centre. Mother went to the kitchen to prepare the food that he had rushed to buy. And I watched the rest of the action movie with my little brother so as to forget about the third sin.

Ten

Honourable Pwagu

The predominantly purple bus bearing Pwagu's party agents and officials now made its way through the mass of eager and cheery supporters who, as early as nine o'clock in the morning, had already filled Freedom Stadium to await morsels of politics from the one man upon whom they could always depend to deliver particularly delectable bits of these. The people had by no means been unaware that Pwagu would arrive here only now, about two o'clock in the afternoon, but to them the thought that Honourable Pwagu was scheduled to deliver an address could not have had them place anything else in their plan for the day. These people, as a matter of fact, attended every other political rally just as dedicatedly; only that Pwagu's had this peculiar way of causing in them great excitement – nay, total ecstasy or even intoxication. They just loved to listen to Honourable Pwagu – whatever it was that he had to say. Well, some attributed this dedication to political rallies to a lack of anything important to do on the people's part; however, the people themselves believed that politics was life itself; that they ate it, drank it, and even swam about leisurely in it. It gave them great pleasure just to listen to verbal attacks and, a while later, responses to the same from those so attacked. Sexual scandals, spouse battering, links to drug dealing and abuse, poor command of formal languages, altercations with ordinary citizens at the citizens' work places owing to haughtiness, pitiable levels of education, court cases, bankruptcy, and such like, did form the basis of attacks at these rallies, and it was such that the people always looked forward to.

And now the main man himself was here, his figure full and firm in a purple shirt meant to hang loose down the sides. He was waving to the people from a convertible car, doing this gently and without even a smile, which contrasted the adoring cheers, shouts, chants and jumps being displayed by the people. A noticeable overall effect of this was that it created something of a reverent aura about him. The convertible moved on at a snail's pace. It now reached the front of the podium and stopped right there. Pwagu stepped out. He headed straight to the centrally placed seat meant for him. The national anthem was sung after which all at the podium got seated while whistling and cheers once again reigned supreme among the people.

The master of ceremonies took the meeting through introductions. Party notables were then called upon to say a word or two. One after the other, they praised the popularity of their party, PDP, and extolled the virtues of Pwagu, their de facto leader. Pwagu's role in the expanding of space for political participation and the nation's democratization in general, one of the speakers said amid cheers, never could be gainsaid.

When Pwagu now rose to his feet, the sounds of horns, whistles, trumpets, drums, and just the sheer power of human voice, rent the air. A whole half a minute elapsed as Pwagu waited for the cheers to die down but they were not about to. He made to open his mouth but stopped. He tried again but stopped again. The adulation carried on. Then amidst it all he now said in a much projected voice, "Alright, alright, honourable citizens," the rich baritone getting borne by the public address system to various corners of Freedom Stadium and outside it. Their being called 'honourable citizens' evoked in the people one wave of elated response: "Yes, Father." Then there was silence, total silence, following Pwagu's clearing his voice purposely for this effect. He went on to say to the now keenly attentive mass of Capital Region dwellers that his heart floated in elation at the knowledge that their support for him and for the party was truly massive, unwavering and unshakeable. He asked them to believe even more in him, saying he had their interests at heart and that only his party had what it took to form the next government, a true government of the people. He promised that if they, the people of Capital Region, gave him their votes and enabled him to become the president of the republic, he would erect, there in the capital, the tallest building in the world, and the next wonder of the world at that. Cheers followed this.

Regarding the apparently fierce competition for the presidency, he noted that he was Shakespeare's Bassanio, on whom the beautiful and honoured Portia had finally settled after a detailed evaluation of all her suitors. They, the people, were the beautiful and honoured Portia and had decisively settled on him, Pwagu, thereby rejecting the other presidential contenders, who could therefore be concluded to be, variously, less appealing, less virile and mere pretenders to the throne. He had to wait for close to another thirty seconds for cheers to die down, for all, including those who had never read any of the legendary writer's works, went wild, holding that it was very intelligent of their leader to speak so creatively, saying such great things straight off the top of his head.

Turning to the incumbent government, led by the president, who was from Southern Region, among the country's most populous tribe, Pwagu said it was not right that the country should be led by the one and same tribe, a tribe only busy amassing wealth and opportunities for itself at the expense of all the others. He told the people that their udders were full of milk, their muscles of energy and their brains of creativity, but that parasites lived on them and inside them, availing themselves of the wonderful products leisurely, products that needed to be of benefit to their owners first and as of right. They did this ungratefully; and eventually left the people deprived and diseased. By voting him, the true father and friend of the people, Pwagu said emphatically, waving his index finger in the air, the incumbent parasites would effectively have been made to drop dead from the bodies of the hardworking and highly productive citizens, who would then have a chance to be free and to enjoy the fruit of their labour happily all the way.

This now intoxicated the people, and they let out shouts of "President Pwagu! President Pwagu! President Pwagu!"

And Pwagu always knew well enough to stop his speech while it was still interesting, and he now did just that, leaving the people wishing for more. As the powerfully built leader of parliamentary opposition made to lower himself to his seat, the people actually shouted, "Tell us more!" But, of course, they now had to go home. As it were, they had had a bite of politics, a good bite of it for that day.

The confidence with which Pwagu had spoken at Freedom Stadium was nothing new; only that today it had belied greatly the worried man that he was deep down. Now with his wife inside their bedroom, Pwagu displayed the full extent of his political and personal worries.

"Darling, what does this woman want?" he posed to his wife there beside him in reference to Miss Mimi, who had since left Pwagu's party, claiming that her conscience and principles never could allow her to continue being a member and secretary general of the Purple Democratic Party.

"Indeed, what does she want?" Mrs. Pwagu threw back the question to her man, tilting her head in his direction there on the bed.

"What will it profit her publishing a book that attacks my integrity?"

"Not a soul will believe whatever she says in that book of hers."

"She has called it *Spilling the Beans: A Journey to Honest Leadership*."

"Betrayal – I call it."

"Our most frequent visitor, darling."

"Yeah, a family friend! Her favourite seat was the one next to the window. Oh, damn the food I prepared for her in this very house. The very first time you had told me only that an honourable friend of yours was coming over, and I got very busy with preparations."

"I remember. You got green with jealousy when you finally saw her, didn't you?"

"I got over it as soon as I got to know her, didn't I?"

"That is true, darling."

"She was a no-nonsense woman, I immediately realized."

"Yeah, she kept her dealings strictly formal. Party affairs were handled just as strictly. Actually, some in our party ranks thought her too much of a perfectionist, such a stickler for rules."

"And a fierce defender of the PDP's reputation. As a matter of fact, Miss Mimi has been a perfect defender of yours – you personally."

"Especially on the matter of the Northern Region Tea Factory."

"A hot political potato – that factory matter – should serious attention be brought to it."

"She says she has written every piece of detail concerning it."

"But why, darling, why? Why does she have to do this?"

"It beats me."

"Let us sleep. This is a storm; but as I say, the storm will surely pass."

"She'll pay for this."

"Lose no sleep over it, darling."

"She'll have to pay for this dearly."

"Good night."

"Night."

Pwagu spent the next week more or less in that apprehensive state of emotion. A lot was at stake, not only with regard to the heavy investment he had made in his presidential campaign but also in respect of his private property. Revelations in Miss Mimi's book could provoke investigations and even embolden certain quarters to institute law suits. His narcotics trade, booming underground, certainly was in the book, as well as the irregularly acquired title deeds of massive tracks of land he held in his native Northern Region.

Miss Mimi now launched her book, *Spilling the Beans: A Journey to Honest Leadership,* at Capital Region University. The public had waited with great curiosity. Supporters of Pwagu had wondered if anyone could be daring enough to stage an affront against their leader whom they loved but at the same time feared owing to the efficiency with which he eliminated any danger to his reputation and political survival in general. His adversaries, of course, had hoped for some juicy stuff that would as well be the mud to sling Pwagu's way so as to spoil his self-declared 'Mr. Clean' image. The waiting was now over. The friends and foes of Pwagu here present were now witnessing the spilling of smelly stuff hitherto unknown to the trusting public.

The author, with rare passion and boldness, left no doubt as to the resolve reflected in the subtitle of her book: that she had embarked on a journey to a destination called honest leadership. If the country's politics was such that citizens did not pay intelligent and critical attention to what their leaders did, she said, there was no hope of growth towards development.

It was a most accomplished presentation, by any standards. She now fielded questions from journalists.

"First, Miss Mimi, receive my sincere congratulations on the successful writing, publication and launch of your book," began First Journalist. "Having said that," he continued, "may I note that whereas I appreciate your having furnished us, as your audience this afternoon, with details as to the motive behind writing *Spilling the Beans*, I wish to ask if you do not think that it will be next to impossible for you to convince even a handful of people that it is no breach of trust exposing someone to whom you have been so close, the truth or otherwise of your writings notwithstanding."

"Thank you for your compliment. May I then say that 'breach of trust' is a legal offence actionable in the court of law – you know that, I'm sure. Now, I am ready to face charges to that effect. But I also know that even amateur thieves have common sense enough not to make their dirty deals formal or public. It'd be, for them, like shooting themselves in the foot."

"You imply that Honourable Pwagu is a – what's the obverse of amateur...er... yes, you imply that Honourable Pwagu is a professional thief."

"Those are your words."

"I know, but this is the implication. Well, let's look at it. First, it is a fact you have worked with him all this time. Now, how can anyone believe that you did not share in the spoils and if, by any chance, you did not, is that then not the reason you are angry, hence the dangerous allegations you make in your book?"

"Even Jesus Christ supped with sinners, much to the chagrin of the Pharisees. Did that make him a sinner himself?"

"Answer that question simply, clearly and honestly."

"I have answered it most simply, clearly and honestly. In any case, honesty is the philosophy of my life."

"But, Miss Mimi," began Second Journalist, "corruption aside, I'm sure even those who support you and your 'journey to honest leadership' would wish to know when it is that you plan to wed."

"Is that the best you can do with a golden chance such as this? Next question?"

"Miss Mimi," began Third Journalist, "one way towards establishing honesty in a society is for us to cultivate that value at the family level. What's your personal view on how we've fared as a nation regarding this and other family values in general?"

"The corrupt of our nation today were once innocent children; and if the instilling of that virtue had taken place, the present rot would not be the case – at least not to its current extent."

"I totally agree; in fact, Miss Mimi, yours would be a model of a family, if what I've just heard from your own mouth be honest. Why then do you not lead by example in the matter?"

"Next question, please."

"You just ignored a question, Miss Mimi."

"I never do that. If indeed I did ignore anything, it must have been only some piece of stupidity, and not a question. I was trained to answer questions very well and I always do my best to give the very best. I hope they trained you too, wherever you learnt journalism, to ask proper questions properly."

"Fine, let us forget about that and move on. Now, do you not fear writing and saying such adverse things about the Honourable Pwagu? Do you really *know* Pwagu?"

"The only thing I fear is fear itself."

"As Roosevelt would say, huh?"

"You are right."

"If you are honest in saying that you have no fear, then it's fine. But then again why only now, when Honourable Pwagu has just embarked on his presidential election campaign? Who, among his competitors, is paying you to do this against a person from your own Northern Region? You northerners are never known to betray your own."

"You see, the kinds of questions you people ask are part and parcel of the big problem in this nation. We need a re-education or something. *Spilling the Beans* gives you information which any serious person would gobble up with all avarice and then interrogate. When is the right time to publish a book, anyway? As a matter of fact, this is the right time – when the power hungry are coming to you with sugar-coated words aimed at taking your attention away from their stinky misdeeds. No one, at all, needs to pay me to do what I am doing. The knowledge that we, as a nation, shall surely attain honest leadership someday is payment enough for me. We all ought to join this quest, making it National Objective Number One! That aside, you forget that I own and run real property and, as such, I am not hungry as a lot of people I know, who go right ahead to sell even their capacity to think."

When there were no more questions, the function came to an end. Beginning the following week, Miss Mimi would tour the other six of the seven regions into which the country was divided – according to tribe and language affinity – on a mission to promote her book, *Spilling the Beans: A Journey to Honest Leadership.*

Pwagu had followed Miss Mimi's book launch on his bedroom television. Oh, his misdeeds were now out there in the eyes of the public.

But, as one of the journalists had remarked, Miss Mimi clearly did not *know* him, he mused. She now would. He was not the kind of politician any man could fool around with; so who did this woman think she was? Clearly, Pwagu said in his heart, Miss Mimi was not in love with her life.

After a weekend spent mostly indoors, yet one that also involved quite a lot of telephone calls, owing to her mission and plans, Miss Mimi was now on her way to Northern Region, her own and Pwagu's region of birth.

The Northern Region headquarters lay quiet, business going on as usual. Deeper into the region, subsistence farmers looked forward to fair harvest of the maize and sorghum crops, unlike the case in previous consecutive seasons. Somewhere even deeper, Northern Region Tea Factory machines rumbled on monotonously, processing harvests from as far as Southern Region.

The lunch time sun shone on the townspeople as they now variously sought eateries, quiet grassy shades, platforms for the spoken word of God and every other way the lunch hour was spent there. And it was just then that Miss Mimi's convoy of vehicles snaked its way into the town. All else came to a standstill. Shouts of "Mimi! Mimi! Mimi!" rent the air. Somewhere or other there could be observed a scuffle among the shouters. The convoy got to the gate of the Town Hall and then into the compound.

Dressed in a white skirt suit, Miss Mimi emerged from her car. A white ribbon held her richly treated curly hair, and shiny black high heels bore her firm fine legs. It was exactly as she had dressed upon her book launch at Capital Region University.

Seated centrally, four members of her team on either side of her, a number of microphones directly in front, Miss Mimi now delved into the substance of her tour. She tackled chosen themes in *Spilling the Beans*, relating each to the dire challenges facing Northern Region. Her audience got awed at her clear grasp of the local issues but waited keenly to hear her mention Pwagu specifically.

She now did that. She told her audience that the northerners' blind and fanatical following of such a crooked leader as Pwagu was the trouble with the leadership of Northern Region. "You have to make up your minds," she said. "You have to resolve that from now on, you shall ask relevant questions about anyone, I mean anyone, who leads or seeks to lead you. Otherwise, they will certainly take advantage of your ignorance to exploit and manipulate you while all the while you yap about at such a leader's greatness which is not greatness at all. I am hitting very hard at this matter, I know, and this is because it is important to you and to the nation at large."

Her passionate expression sent the hall into awed silence, and as she now paused, the effect got truly intense. With fervour so great that a blood vessel now appeared prominently on her neck, she went on: "Unless official impropriety is taken head-on and exposed as I am now doing with regard to Pwagu, Northern Region and indeed the entire nation risks sinking deeper and deeper into the mire of stagnation."

It was at that point that a shoe was flung her direction from among the members of the audience in the fully packed Town Hall. She nearly successfully ducked it but it caught her left shoulder on its way past her, getting deflected a little, so that it got stopped by the chest of one of her guards. Within no time, it was mayhem at the table of presentation as a group from among the audience now surged to the front and there pushed decorative flowers off the table, tore up Miss Mimi's written speech and the copy of *Spilling the Beans* that she had in her hand for purposes of demonstration. As Miss Mimi attempted to rise and run to safety, the leg of her chair caused her to trip and fall to the floor. A few of the goons chuckled at the brief sight of her yellow underpants as a guard helped her rise to her feet.

Tear gas now filled the hall as people scrambled for their way out through the main entrance as well as through the windows. Miss Mimi and her people were led out through the back door, Town Hall security guards now forming a tight human shield around them.

For three good hours, Miss Mimi and her team remained holed up in the town clerk's office as skirmishes went on between supporters of Pwagu and those of Leshom, the only other presidential hopeful to arise out of Northern Region. A man who worked his way from humble peasant background to medical distinction, Leshom was the very first northerner to pose a serious challenge to Pwagu for Northern Region leadership. His Patriotic Party was making inroads quite significantly in all of the republic's seven regions. So serious was the rivalry between these two that almost anything could be turned into a powerful point of difference and an excuse for violence, and this was now the case here. If *Spilling the Beans* criticized Pwagu, Pwagu's supporters held, then the book, its author, and those who associated with her, could only be enemies of Pwagu. It was clear the disruption of the promotion of Miss Mimi's book as well as this confrontation had been premeditated, even pre-planned.

Addressing the press upon arriving back in Capital Region later that evening, Miss Mimi said that the unfortunate disruption of her function in Northern Region only energized her and strengthened her resolve to go all the way in exposing duplicity and corruption till the nation would attain honesty. The vestiges of the intolerant and dishonest yester years, she said, would be thrown to the damping site. That would be done by these same citizens that political tricksters loved to dupe. This would surely happen once the real nature of the crooks was made known to the people most vividly.

Pwagu's party held its next presidential campaign rally, this time in Northern Region. As was always the case, citizens were very much in time for the address by Pwagu and were at this primary school's sports grounds in their numbers this Saturday afternoon. Expectedly, evidence was everywhere that it was strongly felt that the Honourable Pwagu needed to respond to *Spilling the Beans*, which had so far been promoted in four regions – in what its author had termed the first leg of the book's promotion. Aside from the violence witnessed here in Northern Region a while before, Miss Mimi's tours had been uneventful in Western Region, Eastern Region and, most recently, Southern Region, the southerners actually giving her quite a hearty welcome.

So, today placards read: Hon. Pwagu, Do Dismiss the Miss. A huge canvass, borne by six young men, read thus: She's Gonna Eat Her Spilt Beans Today!

It was towards the end of his address that evening that Pwagu made reference to Miss Mimi, this being but the second time he was doing this, having, earlier on, only responded to a journalist's question on the same subject back in Capital Region, saying that though aggrieved, he valued more everyone's constitutional right to express whatever in whatever manner. Now terming Miss Mimi a person of no consequence, he caused wild cheers when he added that his attention was worth only serious things and not the wild imaginations of one woman who needed a husband whom to keep warm and children to keep her wandering mind busy.

With that Pwagu got back to his seat. The rally ended. As the crowd tore away, Miss Mimi was the subject of conversations, pretty mean things being said about her, laughter and staggering characterizing the animated exchanges.

After a week's break, Miss Mimi resumed her regional book promotion tours, the second leg, as it were. Under tight security this time round, she got into South Eastern Region, North Western Region and, finally, Capital Region, where the launch had been done.

A day after Miss Mimi's book promotion tour of Capital Region, an incident occurred. It was at about six o'clock in the evening. As she was being chauffeured from her suburban home to the Capital Mall, unknown gunmen sprayed her vehicle with bullets, leaving her and her driver for dead. The gunmen then disappeared into the nearby forest.

Sympathizers had the two rushed to hospital. Just upon arrival there, unfortunately, Miss Mimi's driver was pronounced dead. His boss struggled on for her life in the hospital's operating theatre, where doctors were racing against time to dislodge bullets from her forehead, left shoulder and her nape, hoping against hope to keep her alive.

This shooting incident made the campaign period truly tense. As Miss Mimi lay in hospital, and the election date drew nigh, pressure mounted on Pwagu to come out clear on the shooting incident. His fellow presidential candidates used this to their advantage, terming the incident as demonstrative of the sort of country they did not want anymore, as they were fed up with repressions, suppressions and assassinations. This was from Leshom. He added that Miss Mimi's shooting was a classic case of corruption fighting back in a deadly way and that the only guarantee to a good nation was the elimination of crooks and murderers through the power of the vote.

Leshom went on to win that presidential election, and one of his first executive actions was to establish a commission of inquiry into the Miss Mimi shooting. The new president had Pwagu placed in detention for the reason that he would be important in supplying critical information in the investigation. Riots rocked the country following Pwagu's detention but the president forced order and normalcy in the country after three ugly days.

Looking back, it was not easy to believe that the once mystically powerful Pwagu, the darling of the people and master of political games, could be reduced to this: a detained presidential loser whom many court cases awaited in the free world outside.

Six months since her admission to hospital, Miss Mimi noted with gladness that *Spilling the Beans* had planted courage in many a heart, for she was now receiving get-well-soon messages from two men seated by her hospital bed speaking of what inspiration she had all along been to them. They showed her copies of books they had written and published within that period, inspired, they reported, by the candour and courage of *Spilling the Beans: A Journey to Honest Leadership*. They assured Miss Mimi of great company in that patriotic journey.

Holding the two books and looking at their titles, Miss Mimi smiled brightly. "I see, the journey continues," she said. She looked at the books further, saying nothing. Then, handing the books back to their owners, she said: "When we shall have created sufficient honesty around, I'll consider running for the presidency."

The gentlemen rose in order to leave, telling Miss Mimi to get well fast for they missed her in the fight against corruption. She responded that she would. As her visitors got out, she got back to a lying position, smiling to herself, her eyes staring at the roof of the hospital ward.

Eleven

Lovers of Wives

An economically worded phone call from Rosalind instantly cleared my morning clogging of mind, sight and voice. The weight and urgency of the message tossed me out of bed and made me frantic, even clumsy. She needed me urgently and with a solution! I asked Jessie for things I did not really expect her to rise and give me as I could just get them myself. These included my jacket and pair of shoes. In record time I put these on and left the house.

And now my branching to Nelson's place, instead of going straight to where I was needed, gave me two strongly contradicting feelings: that I was making a mistake in the way I was responding to an urgent call, and that I actually needed to do this so as to add value to my response, to make myself truly useful to Rosalind when I got to her.

Well, I got to Nelson's house. I pressed the doorbell switch. Silent seconds passed, during which I felt a stirring inside my bowels owing to the distress that had been so palpable in Rosalind's tone in that urgent call from her.

Nelson opened the door. Security lights showed me a face that was both a little sleepy and rather quizzical about my presence here at such an unlikely hour.

I moved straight to the questions that had formed in my mind since the sound of Rosalind's voice had hit my eardrums in that urgent call.

"Nelson," I started, "what is it that would have you *divorce* Nancy, your sweet wife and mother of your three wonderful children?"

"Adultery," he answered, his voice revealing that he had quickly searched through his mind and settled upon marital infidelity as the best answer to the question.

Nelson's voice failed to convince me that he would actually divorce Nancy if Nancy made love with anyone other than him, her husband. So I pursued the same question further, keeping the other questions of mine compactly piled in my mind's abeyance. Nelson knew that I loved to have my questions answered deeply, not just in some standard, perfunctory or routine way.

"You would divorce the mother of your three children if she made love with someone other than you?" I asked, stressing the words 'made love'.

"Nancy cannot do that to me, Janam. Would Jessie do that to you?" he responded, clearly not relishing thoughts along the lines of such a possibility where his wife was concerned.

"Very well, Nelson. I am not here to cause you to doubt your wife's capacity to stay perfectly faithful to you. Neither am I here to shake your fundamental beliefs concerning grounds for divorce. I only seek clarity of understanding, especially for my own sake and for the sake of people about whom I care a lot. To be sure, I know it feels bad to know that someone to whom you make love also makes love to another person or other people. But, Nelson, divorce is devastating! Its effects are massive, practical, far-reaching. The children – their custody, care, emotions and attitude towards life as a result of their parents divorcing! The public – the evil and sadistic interest that they take in watching the drama of your marital struggles and their silent wish that it should all come down crumbling! The court battles – having to divide your property, pay for the maintenance of the person you are kicking out of your life…"

"Listen, Janam. All those things you are mentioning are exactly what ought to give a marital partner every reason to be faithful," said Nelson, cutting me short.

"So if a partner messes up, knowing all this, there should be no excuse. Is that so?" I said.

"Exactly," he said this fast, his conviction evident.

"Is this idea of faithfulness a requirement only on the female partner?" I further pursued.

"No," he said.

"I am posing this simple question to a friend of mine, to a man I know. That makes the question a very serious one, Nelson," I said.

"Well…" he hesitated, realizing what I, a confidant of his, was alluding to.

"Never mind, Nelson," I said. "Allow me to ask a different question: What would you tell someone who has decided that he or she is going to take away his or her life?"

"Who has decided so, Janam? Why such sorts of questions?"

"It's Rosalind. Help me out very fast, Nelson. I ought not to have come here even. From the tone of Rosalind's voice in her phone call to me moments ago, I ought to have headed straight to where she is."

"What exactly is the happening, Janam?"

"Rosalind is shattered. Utterly shattered! Her husband has filed a divorce case in the court of law. The father of such a fine boy and girl in their pubescence! He has evidence, gathered by his private detectives, that Rosalind has a lover, a well-built man in his mid-twenties. She does not understand why her husband is making such a big deal out of her love affair yet he himself, she says, is not blameless in the same regard."

"She has never caught her husband, has she?"

"Nelson, that question is very bad, especially given that it comes from a person of your caliber. Is faithfulness about not being caught or staying true to vows? Oh, maybe I am being too hard on you. I think I would do well to treat that question as part of your admission that marital fidelity is such a hard nut to crack."

"Well, that is fair enough. You know, Janam, we have to set ideals for ourselves in life. We may fail to live up to them, but so long as we try, that is good enough. It is better than having no ideals at all."

"Thank you, Nelson. Talking to you has been more useful to me than you may realise. I shall now rush to where Rosalind is."

"But why are you so much concerned about the whole thing, Janam?"

"I should be – I'll answer that later, Nelson."

And while the steel door of Nelson's house hit the frame shut, I launched myself again in the course, to where Rosalind's urgent call required me. 'Come quickly to the steel bridge' had been the last words of that phone call, Rosalind's urgent early morning call. The steel bridge, which was but a stone's throw from Rosalind's home, helped people cross River Kakoth up in the north, where the river valley was very deep and velocity very high especially in a rainy season such as this one.

The morning mist still limited visibility to about a hundred metres. My shirt felt very cold – as if wet even – upon my body; but if Rosalind was out there, there was nothing for me to grumble about. This fair woman, Rosalind, had once given me a surprise visit in my humble abode and presented me with a painting on which she had worked diligently for six consecutive weeks. It was a wonderful painting of me receiving a trophy.

And when I got near the appointed place, when the steel bridge came into view, I saw two people standing there. I got closer. The man and the woman gave me a vacant look, a look that told me, "Come right to the balustrade and see for yourself."

And indeed there was Rosalind, below the bridge, upon the bank, in a royal blue dress, lying prostrate.

"Let's find our way down there," I said to the man and woman I had found at the steel bridge.

Their travelling bags supported upon their backs, they followed me as I tried to find a winding way to where Rosalind lay. I prayed that she should be not only alive but also able to talk to me so that I may share with her words that would possibly turn around her outlook on life.

But the reality was there for me to face. Rosalind was dead!

Rosalind had taken away her life. She had left beside her lovely body the evidence that she had done this. A little bottle labelled 'Human Poison', emptied of its contents, lay beside her body. A note she left, written in red ink, had just three rather enigmatic words: lovers of wives.

And to date whenever I look at the painting that Rosalind had made of me receiving a trophy, and the urgent phone call she had given me that fateful morning, and my branching to Nelson's place instead of getting straight to where I was needed to offer what help I could, I feel a strong sense of duty to tell the tragic story of Rosalind and to try and explain what she had meant by 'lovers of wives'.

Twelve

The Absent Beauty

Long long ago, when the people of Kakoth still went about in nothing but loin cloths, there arose an urgent need to find a suitable bride for a prince whose father and king had passed away mysteriously in his sleep. Memories of the good king's sudden demise and of detailed funeral rituals that had been accorded him were yet very fresh among the people of Kakoth. But ordinary everyday life was picking up, and a big feast for all the people of Kakoth, during which the prince would choose for himself a bride, was part of the indication that life was indeed going on even if there had been such a big loss in the land.

The King's Council duly arranged the feast. Bulls, rams, goats and cocks got slaughtered. Fish, fresh from River Kakoth, got bought and prepared. And now different large cooking vessels were steaming hot, each with a near-solid mass of local bread made from maize meal, sorghum meal and, much more exciting to many people, the flour of these grains mixed with that of cassava.

Everyone in Kakoth was welcome to this feast; and, indeed, everyone came – perhaps except only the dead and the dying. The chief's home became a sea of humanity. The same had been the case not very long before; only that this time round it was about life rather than death.

And food was served. And the people ate. And everyone was well satisfied. Jokes could be heard relating to such levels of satisfaction. Someone suggested that granaries could well be burned down now that they were so full.

So satisfied, the people now could sit and wait to feed their eyes and ears too; for, this was both a big and complete day. Most importantly, they wanted to know who the chief was going to choose as his bride.

Now the expectations of the people of Kakoth about a suitable bride were very simple, clear and straightforward. She had to be beautiful, the form and features of her face possessing this delicately irresistible feminine attractiveness; she had to be pure, not having been intimate with a man; and she had to be from a good background, of known parentage and lineage, devoid of blaring blots in character. To pass this test was to be on one's way to the marital bed. Anything outside of this set of requirements would be regarded as only a small matter.

But there was this upcoming matter of the shape of the bride's breasts. It was gaining currency and was becoming more and more difficult to ignore in Kakoth. As it were, it was becoming more than a small matter. Indeed, Kakoth's superstition seeped its way into this otherwise little matter of the shape of breasts, so that certain shapes were actually linked to ill fortune.

Now, the people of Kakoth thought favourably of three forms of breasts in their daughters: the mango, the avocado and the pawpaw shapes. The closer to any of these shapes a girl's breast was, the more favourable she was in the eyes of the people of Kakoth. A definite and full mango, avocado or pawpaw won complete favour straightaway. Mere pretenses to these ideal shapes caused one to be taken a little less seriously, while those which were far removed from the ideal expectations missed out altogether on the joy of winning worthy attention. And, speaking of shapes that were far removed from the ideal, there was this breast shape which the people of Kakoth compared to the fruits of a tree locally known as *Yago*. Any daughter of Kakoth would be truly uneasy if her breasts so much as evoked the image of the fruits of this tree called *Yago*. *Yago* was ubiquitous in Kakoth, and the sight of it alone just made a daughter of Kakoth truly self-conscious. None could like her foremost feminine features being associated, even jokingly, with the longish, dangling fruits of *Yago*.

So now there the girls were, in front of the multitude. They were the most beautiful and self-confident of all the daughters of Kakoth, ready to show Prince Sunday what their mamas gave them, as it were. Prince Sunday had assumed leadership all right, but he would change titles and be known as King Sunday only upon joining up with a suitable daughter of Kakoth as his wife, the one who would bear the future ruler of the great people of Kakoth.

The maidens walked before the eyes of the prince in the best way their mothers and female relatives had taught them, each time clad in some purposely designed attire. Then they sought to prove the suppleness of their waists by letting themselves loose in dance. Each danced to the drumbeats and tunes of Kakoth, seeking not just to do it well but to outdo all the rest and win Prince Sunday over to herself. And this seemed to be the climax of the show, going by how glued to the scene everybody was. No wonder the people of Kakoth loved to say that one's power is in one's waist.

The maidens, as well, were subjected to a question-and-answer session, which was meant to enable the prince to gauge the sweetness of voice and aptness of mind of each of these maidens from among whom a mother of his children was expected to come.

Indeed the prince saw and heard nothing but feminine greatness in these daughters of Kakoth who had shown themselves off before him. The elders were well pleased, as was clear in the address that one of them was now delivering to the huge gathering to mark the end of the display of beauty and talent. The elder thanked the parents of Kakoth for such great upbringing of daughters, who were not only healthy but also admirably knowledgeable in the important matters and ways of Kakoth. As to their amazing beauty, the elder said while shaking his head affectedly, the rulers of Polo, who made the people of Kakoth, apparently never had any business at all with ugliness. And he added that he was sure that the prince's heart, where he sat, was well pleased and that he had made his choice, which he would now rise and make known to the people.

Prince Sunday rose. He opened his mouth and began to speak. He said to the huge gathering that his heart could not be pleased at all when Nyamami was not among those who had presented themselves for him to choose from. Having said that, he resumed his seat, leaving everyone suspended in unbelievable confusion.

The elders all rose at once. They were furious. Fine, they had not been unaware of the fact that the prince had feelings for the girl in question, this girl called Nyamami; but it had never occurred to them that the prince could choose to disregard tradition and traditional standards that guided choice of a bride for a son of Kakoth, and especially a prince and king-in-waiting, such as he was. And to put them to such public shame! They were the King's Council, the life-long advisors of his father!

A man of his own mind, decisive almost to a fault, Prince Sunday went ahead and married the girl that he had chosen according to his own personal standards and taste, this girl called Nyamami. Nyamami had been brought along by her mother when her mother married the man who was to become the father of her other children and beloved husband. Nyamami's mother had firmly told her not even to think of appearing at the big feast alongside the other fair maidens of Kakoth, for she could expose her to shame, especially if she were to go on to win over the other girls.

As the people of Kakoth loved to say, a prominent position does not change a person, it reveals a person. Nyamami now stood revealed to the people of Kakoth. Not very long after becoming Prince Sunday's queen, the people already were discovering great things about her that made them love her.

And as Nyamami's nature got revealed more and more, the new king became more and more revered. He knew how to chose, the people said in small conversations.

So the king's judgment on matters came to be loved and valued like gold. From the very beginning of his reign it was not difficult at all to see that he would be even greater than his father.

And never had a woman been as wise as Nyamami was now proving to be. Never had a wife brought such honour to her husband as Nyamami now did. She loved the people her husband led, and came up with initiatives that sought to make these people's lives as happy as possible. Among the first things she did was to start a tailoring and design school for the young people of Kakoth. Kakoth Women Saving and Lending Scheme was another. As these thrived and expanded, Nyamami came up with and implemented many more ideas that filled the people of Kakoth with great joy.

And this king ruled wisely till his death, when his eldest son with Queen Nyamami succeeded him.

Thirteen

Black Café

Sizzling mouthwateringly in hot oil were potato chips; rotating slowly in the grilling heat were whitish brown bodies of broiler chickens plucked naked. The air smelled good indeed.

And from the door of the kitchen section of this downtown cafeteria, Ajifu Akiko surveyed her workers and felt pleased. Some held long-handled draining spoons, studying carefully the chips in the sea of hot oil, looking for that colour and visual texture that indicated to them, as culinary experts, that the chips were ready and very well done. Others gripped grilled chickens with implements and cut them up fast and skillfully into pieces that would then be sold as 'quarter-chicken' or 'half-chicken'. Yet others prepared lettuce, watercress, tomatoes, onions, aubergine and a host of other vegetables meant for salad. Ajifu Akiko then went back to the counter, at the entrance of the cafeteria, where orders and payments were made.

"Welcome, sir," said Ajifu Akiko enthusiastically to a customer who had entered just as she took her place at the counter. The gentleman sneered, looking around at nothing in particular.

"I can't see anyone here to serve me," he said to Ajifu Akiko without allowing any eye contact with her, the sneer never leaving his face.

"I am here to serve you, sir," Ajifu Akiko said earnestly.

"I guess I'm in the wrong place then," said the gentleman as he turned and started on his way out, leaving Ajifu Akiko quite startled.

Ajifu Akiko wondered what was wrong. But just then three women happened by.

"Gosh! What's this at the counter?" the tallest of them mumbled highly nasally to his companions.

"An orangutan – I suppose," nasalized another as they all turned to look outside.

"I know the food here is good," said the shortest and apparently the youngest of them.

"Oh, please!" the one who had spoken first retorted disapprovingly. "Let's get out of here," she added, leading the way out.

And just like that they left Ajifu Akiko's fast food place.

It was more or less the same pattern the rest of the day. In fact, only a handful had taken seats at Ajifu Akiko's cafeteria to have the delicious food prepared there.

Now Ajifu Akiko was back to her house. She settled on the sofa to watch the evening news. A minister's statement in parliament was played over and over again. Studio interviews and interactive sections of bulletins were about nothing but that minister's remarks.

Honourable McFilth had commented in parliament earlier in the day that the country had to be very careful, for an orangutan could only promote the interests of fellow orangutans, and, soon enough, they would dominate over the true children of the land. It had been a heated debate. It was all about immigration laws, as contained in a Bill prepared by

Immigration and Integration Minister, Donna Kwajulu, a human rights attorney and first-generation immigrant citizen. She had had her university education here in the country, found work and secured citizenship.

Ajifu Akiko now had everything in proper perspective. That term 'orangutan'! It was what a customer had mumbled there before, wasn't it? So, her skin colour was the matter, wasn't it? This explained why business was always good when Ashley was at the counter – which, thankfully, was the case most of the time. But, wait a minute. The cafeteria was hers – Ajifu Akiko's, that is. Through it she had given opportunity to all those young-stars who worked there, so that they may earn themselves some pounds – you know, for their pockets, for college and suchlike. And they all loved and respected her. They appreciated her so much for this and for everything about her – her way with words, her constant smile, her love for good dressing and all.

Ajifu Akiko placed her legs stretched out on the sofa and covered them with a piece of woolen cloth. She thought of her workers. As she surveyed them earlier that day, she had felt a unique sense of humanity in herself. To be able to be of such use to others in life! To be able to empower young people! It did not matter whether they were of her race or not. Each of them there, black or white, had found something to do, courtesy of her cafeteria, and they were grateful for this. How would they feel if they heard that someone was trying to belittle the sweet lady to whom they referred simply and fondly as 'M'am'?

So, it pained her very much to know that there were people in this country who still harboured mentalities of centuries past. A government minister, in this day and age, still judge people by the colour of their skin.

What Ajifu Akiko did first thing the following morning was to contact a painter, the same man who always did for her that kind of work. She instructed the painter to replace the name 'Fine Food Café' with 'Black Café', and to make a signboard reading 'Food Nice, But We're Black'.

The painter did as instructed. The name change came first and very fast, so that by about nine o'clock, 'Black Café' stared boldly at those approaching the restaurant. 'Black Café' was the new name of Ajifu Akiko's cafeteria, and this was noted with great curiosity.

A little later in the day, the painter delivered the signboard. Wonderful was the work of his hand. Ajifu Akiko stationed it just outside the entrance of the cafeteria. And every day, upon opening business, the first thing the workers were to do was to place the signboard outside there.

And within a matter of days, Ajifu Akiko's cafeteria was registering double sales; I mean double what Ashley herself had been making. It no longer seemed to matter who it was that stood at the counter.

Fourteen

Twin Sisters

Tambo asked Miranda, his wife and mother of their twin daughters, if she was ready. The mother of Terry and Tabby gave herself a final look in the mirror and, satisfied with how she looked, said to her husband, "Ready, honey!" They had an appointment at their daughters' school.

And so they left the house, earlier than usual this morning. They preferred to attend to their children's school matters together, unless it was absolutely impossible for the both of them to make it. Tambo would create time, and from his bank office drive to his wife's business premises, pick her up and then drive to where their attention was required. This morning they were leaving from the house, as their appointment was scheduled for eight o'clock.

So now they were on the road. The highway had not many vehicles yet. The two had determined that they should leave so early so as to elude the usual traffic snarl up that otherwise would have had them spend up to some precious three quarters of an hour just to get to the other side of the city's central business district.

And the windscreen wipers of their Subaru swept from side to side, clearing the mild morning mist. Headlights shone to alert any on-coming vehicle of an approaching car in the early morning poor visibility.

Once on the other side of the city's central business district, and some distance from it, Tambo and Miranda got to a motel. They had breakfast. After that, they did a few more kilometers and got to their daughters' school.

The two were in time for the appointment. From the parking lot they headed straight to the head teacher's office, the ambience of which both of them already could feel, somehow, owing to their familiarity with the place. They made gentle steps upon the pavement leading to the office, which was a nice spacious room. Two potted climbing plants at the far corners of the office caught one's attention upon one's getting in.

Mrs Gatu was of course there and ready to receive these parents whom she liked very much owing to their united approach to their children's school affairs. She would have loved to share the story of this couple's approach with many a parent but for the kinds of kids Terry and Tabby were. These girls were a complete opposite of their gentle, dutiful and straightforward parents. Indeed, it was because of a series of Terry and Tabby's instances of misconduct that their parents had been asked to be here today. Mr and Mrs Tambo were to show how best their daughters could be helped.

"Good morning, Mr and Mrs Tambo," said the head teacher.

"Good morning, Mrs Gatu," responded Terry and Tabby's parents together.

"Now," continued Mrs Gatu, "may I take you straight to the heart of the matter. Your daughters are reckless, violent and arrogant. That is the true picture. If we will find a way of overcoming these, then this meeting will not have been in vain. The girls will have been helped. Please take a look at these letters first."

Mr and Mrs Tambo took the letters. They took cursory glances at the love letters written to their daughters.

Now Mr Tambo shook his head as his eyes ran across the lines that read:

> *...you are well accommodated in my warm heart. Actually, without either of you, half of my heart would have remained unoccupied...*

Mrs Tambo felt as if she would fall to the floor as she read there silently. She could not believe that what she was reading had been written to her daughters, her innocent daughters, as she liked to think of them. Emotion twitched in her lips when she came to the lines:

> *...Sweethearts, as far as I am concerned, you two are one; and I will always love you as such. Indeed, according to what I was recently taught, you two actually began life as one. My love for you, therefore, is meant to have you live life as you had begun it: together. I love you, Terry and Tabby, and I want...*

She turned to the second letter in her hand. Scanning through it, she contorted her face at various points. Fury simmered inside her. These now were her daughters' words in response to the letter from the good-for-nothing boy, who had signed off as:

> *'Your chips and chicken,
> Raphael'.*

Well, Mrs Gatu called the two parents' attention. She informed them that those letters had been found in the girls' boxes during a dormitory inspection exercise. She added that what they were getting concerning their daughters was only the tip of the iceberg; that she had much more information concerning the girls and their conduct inside and outside school.

"About this chips-and-chicken boy – " said Mrs Gatu, "your daughters decided that they must have the same boyfriend – forget, first, about my constant counsel to the entire student body that they must steer clear of such relationships in the very first place. Yet this is not the worst of Terry and Tabby. Whenever they happen to cause trouble, I tell you, it is double trouble.

And, at this juncture, I wish to call them here, just so that you may get to see and hear them talk about this 'chips and chicken boy' as well as a host of other troubles that they have caused here in school and outside."

Mr Tambo cleared his throat and said with a sigh, "Children! Children!"

And Mrs Gatu picked up the telephone receiver and asked her secretary, on the other end of the telephone, to come over.

And in no time at all the secretary came by. Mrs Gatu sent the beautiful young lady, with a note, to go and call Terry Tambo and Tabby Tambo, both of Form Two South, to her office. The parents scanned through the letters in their hands some more in the meantime, absolutely shocked that such things were going on.

After a short while, two healthy-looking girls of striking resemblance walked into the head teacher's office. It was Tabby in front. Different expressions flickered upon her face. It was the same case with Terry, for naturally they felt good to see their parents but then again were seriously anxious about this particular summon to the head teacher's office. They stood in there, their eyes showing that they were wondering what on earth they should do, and especially whether it would be okay for them to greet their parents without their stern head teacher's green light.

"Greet your parents," Mrs Gatu said to them.

Terry and Tabby shook their parents' hands and then resumed their standing positions. For seconds there was silence in the office as Mrs Gatu jotted down something. The girls' eyes looked round, from one part of the office to another. Tension filled them to the brim.

"Now, girls," began Mrs Gatu, looking at the sisters, "you are aware that your parents are here on account of your unbecoming conduct. First, explain, as your parents listen, why you insulted your class prefect."

"We did not insult her, madam," said Tabby, the quicker and more volatile of the two.

"If I say you insulted your class prefect, then you did. Explain what it was all about," said Mrs Gatu.

"She took our letter," said Terry determinedly.

"What sort of letter was it and why did your class prefect take it from you?" said Mrs Gatu.

"It was our letter, written to us by our boyfriend," said Tabby.

"How many times have I talked to you students about that idea of boyfriends? By the way, what do you mean 'our boyfriend' – you and who?" fumed Mrs Gatu.

"And Terry," said Tabby, butting her eyelids once.

"One boy for both of you?" said Mrs Gatu.

"A lot of people do not understand this," explained Tabby, "but Terry and I are one. We were conceived together, were in the womb together, were born together and all. We do our stuff together."

"Are you serious? There has got to be something wrong with you, girls!" said Mrs Gatu. "Seriously, Mr Tambo…" she added, turning to look at the girls' father, while her hand gestured at the girls.

"Terry and Tabby," said Tambo, "I am ashamed of you. Mrs Gatu, I do not understand what has come of these children. I do not know where they get such ideas."

"And you are shameless enough, Tabby, to repeat such nonsense before us!" put in their mother.

"Tabby, you boasted to your class prefect that you beat her in English all the time, and that for that matter she had no authority to take away your letter?"

"I did not boast, madam."

"Okay, you said the truth, huh?"

"Well, I…"

"Very well. So, if it had been someone who beats you in English, it would have been all right for them to take your letter, right?"

"No. It would not have been all right."

"You were only trying to cut your class prefect down to size, I see. Now tell me. Stems of *miraa* were found in your box during the dormitory inspection. How did those things end up in your box?"

"I bought them when we went out for the hockey competition. I was told by the seller that they are good for keeping one awake if one wants to study for some extra hours, for example after evening preps."

"But the school rules do not permit you to carry drugs into the school compound. And you know that."

"Those things help me when I need to work extra hard, when I feel I have not done enough."

"So, you are creating your own rules which you are following conveniently."

Tabby went silent. The head teacher turned to Terry and said, "Terry, you are yet to tell me why you have decided to disregard my counsel against students having love relationships."

"Raph – excuse me – Raphael loves us, and we love him too," said Terry.

"What do you know about love at that age of yours?" fumed Mrs Gatu.

"Madam, Raph loves me and Tabby; and that is how it is meant to be. That is how it will be, for life."

"Relax, young lady. Not so fast, relax. Now, you two insulted a Form Four girl together, you and your sister – one taking over from where the other had left off, unleashing invectives and so forth. Offensive language is not permitted in school, and of this you are aware."

"She started it, madam. That girl had said we were not beautiful enough to win Miss Earth Beauty Contest. No one had even invited her to our discussion!" said Terry.

"But, surely, is that such an important thing that it should cause a quarrel?" put in Mrs Tambo.

"It was the way she said it. She was trying to demean us, you know?" said Terry.

And at that point Mrs Gatu released the girls, so that she may get to confer a little more with their parents.

"Mr and Mrs Tambo, I could be mistaken but I have a very strong feeling that you two may not be keeping sufficiently close contact with your daughters. I certainly like their fearlessness and free self-expression. If only they received closer check – you know, monitoring of what they feed their minds upon! For instance, this idea that they are twins and so they have to do things together, including having the same boyfriend – I mean…"

"It must be *that* so-called boyfriend of *theirs*. He has totally confused their thinking with silly ideas from – from God-knows-where," put in Mrs Tambo, biting her lips in anger.

"That, Mrs Tambo, is the more reason you, as the parents, need to be much closer to the girls than you think you are. Here in school, we are trying our best; and, as you can see, every one of the many cases in which they are involved surely comes to our attention, and we do what is expected according to school rules and our responsibility. You two really impress me by your turning up together for meetings and school events; however, that, certainly, is not enough. What the children read or watch on the screen, the company they keep, the sorts of conversations they engage in, and all, are very significant in influencing their outlook and approach to life, especially such quick minded children as Terry and Tabby.

So, please take the girls with you. Stay with them at home for some two weeks. They will miss quite a bit, but it will sink well in their minds that the way they have conducted themselves, on very many occasions, is indeed unacceptable in the society that we are trying to make. Bring them back after that duration, and I am absolutely sure there will be a big difference."

So, as it was, Terry and Tabby served the suspension. The period was a sobering one, not only to them but also to their parents, who came to realize that they really might not have been quite in touch with their daughters.

The girls were brought back to school. Indeed, the suspension had made them realise a lot of things which they had hitherto taken for granted. They changed, and now they are among the best-behaved in their school. Above all, there is no doubt that they are going to excel in their education and in life.

www.ingramcontent.com/pod-product-compliance
Lightning Source LLC
Chambersburg PA
CBHW050824180626
46814CB00004B/1453

* 9 7 8 9 9 6 6 1 6 9 3 3 4 *